HEART OF TANGO

ELIA BARCELÓ teaches Spanish Language and Literature at the University of Innsbruck. She has been awarded many prizes for her science fiction, but with *Heart of Tango* she is gaining the wider readership she richly deserves.

DAVID FRYE'S translations include *Thine Is the Kingdom* and *Distant Palaces* by Abilio Estévez, as well as poetry by the Cuban poet Nancy Morejón and non-fiction works on South American politics, art and literature.

"Almost Shakespearean . . . In the 'Guaranteed Satisfaction' range"
JEFF PARK, *Radio 4's Front Row*

"An evocative historical thriller. The lively pace of its plot – built around two dancing couples who are destined to meet on some metaphoric dance floor – drives things along towards a surprising conclusion"
CHRIS MOSS, *Times Literary Supplement*

"Barceló captures perfectly the shoddy edges of [Buenos Aires], the rivalry between neighbourhood tango bands and the clubs where knife-wielding immigrants rub besuited shoulders with well-heeled aristos, all equally smitten with the fashionable new dance"   CHARLIE GARDES, *Time Out*

"The story makes many complicated steps back and forth, leaving the reader dizzy with elation, and enthralled by the possibilities presented"
ALANNAH HOPKINSON, *Irish Examiner*

"An impossibly romantic story . . . Barceló's lyrical prose loses nothing in this translation from her native Spanish"   *Image Magazine*

"This little book is bursting with passion and life"   *Star Magazine*

"A reader may be lost in its passionate, sensuous yet real world, and will not want to put it down. An intriguing and impressive novel"
LYNN GUEST, *Historical Novel Review*

W9-AUE-086

Elia Barceló

HEART OF TANGO

Translated from the Spanish by
David Frye

MACLEHOSE PRESS
QUERCUS · LONDON

First published in Great Britain in 2010 by MacLehose Press
This paperback edition first published in 2011 by

MacLehose Press
an imprint of Quercus
21 Bloomsbury Square
London, WC1A 2NS

Originally published in Spain as *Corazón de tango* by
451 Editores, Madrid, 2007.
Copyright © 2007 by Elia Barceló

English translation copyright © 2010 by David Frye

The moral right of Elia Barceló to be identified as the
author of this work has been asserted in accordance with
the Copyright, Designs and Patents Act, 1988.

David Frye asserts his moral right to be identified
as the translator of the work

A CIP catalogue reference for this book is available
from the British Library

ISBN 978 1 84916 407 8

2 4 6 8 10 9 7 5 3 1

Designed and typeset in Roos by Patty Rennie
Printed and bound in Great Britain
by Clays Ltd, St Ives plc

The squeezebox moans, the light's too bright;
night falls on the dance floor and pretty soon
the shadows are gathering, shades of
Griseta, Malena and Mariester.
The shades the tango drew to the dance
make me recall her, too;
come on, let's dance, it hurts me so
to dream of her shining satin dress.

Whose ghost haunts the violin?
Whose sentimental voice,
tired of long suffering,
has started sobbing like this?
Perhaps it's her voice,
the voice that suddenly
fell silent one day.
Or perhaps it's my drink —
perhaps!
It can't be her voice,
her voice has passed on;
it must be nothing more
than the ghosts in my drink.

Like you, she was far away and pale;
her hair was dark, eyes olive grey.
And her mouth, by the early light of dawn,
was the sad hue of the rose.

One day she failed to show, I waited long,
and then they told me of her end.
That is why the shades of tangos
recall her to me again and again, in vain.

Lyrics to the tango "Tal vez será mi alcohol" ("Perhaps It's My Drink"), later renamed "Tal vez será su voz" ("Perhaps It's Her Voice"). Lyrics by Homero Manzi (Homero Nicolás Manzione Prestera), music by Lucio Demare, first recorded on 6 May, 1943. It was later sung by Libertad Lamarque in a version written for a woman, in which she recalls a man:

Like you, he was far away and pale;
his hair was dark, eyes olive grey.
And his hands were smooth and his verses sad,
like the keening of this violin.

ONE

I met her at a milonga on an April night when the wind gusted with the fury of cyclones, carrying on its back the scent of the river and the damp forests, dark and menacing, that surrounded the small mountain city where my work had once more led me.

It was past eleven when I arrived, and as soon as I opened the door the atmosphere inside was almost enough to make me turn back to seek the shelter of my hotel and the sleep I badly needed after so many hours stuck at the computer screen, struggling to impose order on the chaos of the company that had contracted my services. But my addiction proved the stronger, and when Gardel's voice hit me, still hesitating on the threshold, with his first words — *If you know how my soul still harbours the love I once felt for you* — I knew I'd stay, at least for as long as Gardel kept singing, for as long as some woman's body might cling to mine in silence and allow itself to be swept away by the tango's witching charms.

Women there were in plenty, as always, spread out against the walls, looking dreamy or hungry, slowly smoking in the nooks and corners of a dance hall dimly lit by a couple of floorlights shining through filters of pink fabric. In the centre, in the open circle between tables, a few couples dressed in street clothes danced solemnly, eyes closed.

It wasn't the first time I'd been to a place like this, a sort of parish church multipurpose room, long tables pushed up against the walls, heap of paper cups and soft drinks in the furthest corner, tall windows trembling and shaking in the night wind. Still, it always moved me to the core to find, even in a small central European city and on a work night, people like me who were ready to give up a few hours of rest to abandon themselves to this music, albeit in an ugly, soulless dance room with a portable player and a pile of C.D.s.

Innsbruck had always struck me as a sad city, maybe because I had always seen it by night, after the sun had set, or early in the morning, before it had risen. A grey city of grey people, as if the weight of their history, of so many dead over so many centuries, formed a kind of tombstone that wouldn't let them lift their eyes, their souls, their voices. At this moment I got the fleeting impression that I was surrounded by ghosts; but tango blurs things, blears things, much as alcohol does, and the ghosts made good company for my nocturnal self, the self I rarely think about by day and that takes full control of me by night at a milonga, that springs up with desire for a time that I have never known, with nostalgia for a woman who never was, waiting for me back in La Boca.

No-one greeted me. As I hung up my raincoat and sat to lace

my dancing shoes, several women's eyes passed over me, attentive, expectant, observing my deliberate and precise motions to measure how skilled my body might be, how fluid my steps across the dance floor, how sure my arms in announcing my desires.

No other civilized activity still exists in which the male of the human species can dictate what he wants, and the woman will follow him, devotedly, confidently, surely. The Argentine tango is the only contract that can never be broken. Perhaps that is why it became my passion on that far-off day when I discovered it on a trip to Buenos Aires.

My nocturnal self — the tango dancer, the milonguero, the self that no-one in my daylight life has met — stood up and once again, through a miracle that astounds me no matter how many times it is repeated, my whole body changed, became aware of its weight, its expertly distributed equilibrium, the soft brushing of the leather soles of my shoes against the polished parquet floor, the firmness of my hips, the way my chest expanded and shone like a beacon, searching for the woman who would reflect its light.

Then I saw her. Standing at the other end of the hall, one shoulder leaning against the jamb of a half-opened door through which filtered a breeze, rippling open the razor-keen slit in her tight, satin skirt to reveal a leg, iridescent in black silk. Smoke rose from a cigarette held in her long, delicate fingers, as if she had forgotten it, by her thigh. She wore high-heeled dancing shoes with criss-crossed buckles.

In the low light I couldn't see her face, which turned outwards as if to see something beyond the door. I could just make out her long black hair, coiled in a tall chignon held in place with an antique tortoiseshell comb sprinkled with tiny stones which, like the gold rings dangling from her ears, glittered in the pink darkness.

She was an engraving torn from an old album, a sepia-toned photograph, a woman whose likes exist only in the stories I used to tell myself at night before sleep, inspired by the verses of tangos. Next to her all the other women suddenly seemed hazy, dispensable, and the concealed passion that might be seen in the bodies of these Central European women for a few dimly lit hours in the dance hall when they forgot their everyday lives as dentists, secretaries, housewives — a poor, wilful passion that I knew so well — was relegated to other nights and other places; pale, dim memories when faced with the dazzling, impossible reality of this woman who seemed to be waiting for me and only me, a stranger blown in by the wind, like in some old movie.

She didn't see me walk over. I don't think she even heard me. But, dropping her cigarette at the first strains of "Volver", she turned towards me and her eyes drank me in. Black eyes, resplendent as mirrors, framed by long lashes. A moment later we were dancing.

It was like flying; like being immersed in deep warm water that throbbed to a rhythm rung by an old, sweet grief, a vague memory lost in time. It was like finding something that I had had to forget in order to keep living, something that filled me now to brimming over with its vastness. It was everything I thought I had been making up all these years, and now it dazzled me in the vividness of its perfect reality.

She clung to me like a silk handkerchief. With every molinete that she twirled around me I was overwhelmed by her scent, the scent of a woman, and her eyes — solemn, stern, half closed in pleasure — sparkled like jewels. It was as if she could read my thoughts, as if she already knew half a second before I hinted at a movement what I was going to ask her to do, and as if her body were bending to my desires, a single body unfolded into two figures and united by music.

We didn't exchange a single word. It wasn't necessary. What could we have said to each other that wasn't already there — in our feet, weaving patterns on the floor; in our bodies, surrendering to that eternal rhythm? Any attempt on my part to speak German would have broken the magic spell, and I was horrified at the idea of speaking to her in Spanish and finding that she could not understand me, or hearing her German accent answer me with a few phrases that she had learned in night classes.

For a moment I thought that she might be a Spanish speaker, that we might be able to escape at some point through the door she had been leaning against, perhaps to smoke a cigarette in an empty garden and chat in our own language. But then would follow the routine of what's your name and what kind of work do you do, the terrible moment of finding out that this splendid woman who danced like a Buenos Aires goddess, as if she had stepped out of a Quinquela Martín painting of docks and tenement life, was merely an Argentine psychologist in exile, or a Dominican woman who sold underwear by day.

Her lips brushed lightly against my unshaven cheek and I knew we were thinking the same thing. That we had come here to dance, that the night was ours, that a miracle of fate had brought us together in the middle of the night, in the centre of Europe, to let ourselves be swept away by the magic of tango. And that this was enough.

We danced one song after another, never stopping — a milonga that enhanced her elegance, a few Pugliese tangos that seemed to surprise her for a moment with their sorrowful, rending wail.

I don't know how long we stayed, because the time that clocks measure is time of a different sort.

At some moment an African boy — one of those street vendors who present you with an enormous bouquet of long-stemmed roses out of nowhere — appeared by our side, displaying a white grin like a gash across a face that looked exhausted from so many rejections, so many couples in expensive nightspots diverting their gaze as soon as he showed up.

She looked at the flowers in fascination, and a wavering smile appeared on her lips, painted in the same deep red as the roses the boy was selling. Without letting go of her waist, I reached into my trouser pocket, took out a couple of bills, and offered them to him with a smile. He took another look at his bouquet, as if it were hard to decide which one to select, picked out a perfect rose that had barely begun to open, and handed it to her. She looked at me, traced her lips with the rose, snapped off the long stem, put the flower in the cut of her dress, closed her eyes and leaned all her weight against me, yielding to my embrace.

We danced. And danced. Ignoring the cheap parish hall, ignoring the dull couples who counted their steps or who announced their moves in an undertone as if they couldn't turn the music into dance without translating it first into words; ignoring the resentful gazes tossed our way by the women standing against the wall; ignoring the clock that somewhere was ticking down the seconds of a night that I wished would never end.

At some point I began to notice the scrape of furniture being moved, a fluttering as of a flock of startled doves; a quick look was all I needed to understand that the milonga was at an end. Couples were putting on their coats, carting off the soft drinks, emptying out the overstuffed ashtrays. Lone women were leaving two by two, accusing me of something with a toss of their heads towards the dance floor before disappearing into the darkness of the entrance way. The music stopped.

I felt her weight in my arms for a few moments, her head on my shoulder, her leg curled around mine. Then, still not speaking, we separated. She glanced towards the door, as if making a plea that I didn't understand at the time, looked again at the rose in her dress, gave me a quick kiss on the cheek, parted from me, and walked out, with the grace of a flowing river, into the dark. Her last, sad, sweet smile seemed to hang in the sudden silence, the sudden loneliness that shook me like a spasm.

I went to change my shoes, put on my raincoat, and waited in the entrance that was lit only by the pearly light of the street lamps, until the last dancers left and locked the dance room with a double turn of the key, a definitive and dismal sound.

I lit a cigarette and waited, looking at the reflection of street lamps on my shoes, glancing furtively in the direction of the ladies' room, where she must be getting ready to go out for a night with a stranger, with me. Go out where?

She must have been feeling as breathless as I, which was why she wasn't coming out; the same sudden desire to flee, to disappear, now that the tango had fallen silent.

A car drove down the lonely street, and its sodden sound made me step over to the door and look out. It had started raining. The gentle rain turned the halos around the street lamps into glittering rainbows and made the asphalt gleam like patent leather. Not a soul to be seen.

I came back inside and, with sudden resolve, rapped my knuckles on the door to the ladies' room. Total silence. I opened the door softly and was startled by the darkness within. It was empty. Not just empty: deserted, abandoned, like a boat left adrift. The way I myself felt.

I returned to the entrance, sat on one of the stone steps and lit another cigarette, though I knew that there was no longer any sense in waiting. She had left.

Had she come without a coat, without a bag, without an umbrella? I made an effort to remember what the dance hall had looked like before I went out to wait for her, thinking that she had just skipped into the ladies' room. It had been empty. There had been nothing there but the C.D.s, which the last couple picked up before they locked the room. And the staircase only led to the ladies' room and the wide entrance way, where I had stood smoking next to the exit.

I went outside into the weary rain which, now that the wind had stopped, was falling almost vertically, and walked with head lowered and hands shoved into my raincoat pockets, back to the old quarter of the city. The night porter gave me the key to my room. I went up and, as always, emptied the pockets of my raincoat and sports jacket on to the dressing table: wallet, passport, keys, business cards, a couple of receipts, and a folded slip of paper that I didn't recognize.

I unfolded it with trembling hands. It was an address in the district of La Boca, Buenos Aires, and a woman's name: Natalia.

* * *

The month of August was already half over and the southern winter was in full swing when I finally managed to reach Buenos Aires. No sooner had I set foot in my hotel room in the city centre than, in a fever of imminence, I scoured the street directory for the address that was engraved in my memory, though the slip of paper so often unfolded had never left me. It was, indeed, an address in the quarter of La Boca, a small side street just two steps from Calle Caminito.

The taxi dropped me off at the corner, in a poorly lit section that, were it not already familiar to me from previous trips, would have seemed dangerous. Despite the cold I wore my dance shoes because, if I didn't find her at home, I knew where I would meet her. I had dreamt this over and over again, in dozens of hotel beds in dozens of cities where my work had led me over the four months since that April night: the taxi would drop me off at the corner, I'd quickly cross over to the address written on the note and knock on her door, which would be locked at that time of night. I'd look up, searching for the light in her window, and then I'd walk down Caminito, empty of tourists, nobody there to gush over its colourfully painted houses and corrugated roofs, and the shine on my shoes would light my path to Los Gitanos, a tiny nightspot with scarcely six tables where they dance a sensual, raffish, local tango. She'd be there, waiting for me, leaning against the door as she had that night, the smoke from her cigarette describing serpentine curls around her wrist, her eyes dark stars inviting me to dance.

It didn't surprise me to find the house locked and no light in the room upstairs. What alarmed me was the abandoned, funereal atmosphere of the boarded-up windows, the rust-covered knocker, the weeds growing on the front steps.

Feeling tightness in my chest, I walked to the milonga, wishing I hadn't left my hat in the hotel, noting how the damp air seeped through the upturned collar of my coat and strove to free my hair from its slick layer of gel.

The notes of the tango filled the street with nostalgia. Four candles burned on the empty tables in the nightspot. By the abandoned bar, a mature couple danced alone with the languid nimbleness of lifelong tangueros.

I stood watching through the window, unable to accept that she wasn't there. I stayed for a long time, hypnotized by the guttering light of the candles, feeling each note of the tango stab me within, until the barman noticed my silhouette and invited me in with a wave of his hand. I shook my head and left as if I were being pursued, running away from my failure, and walked for hours through deserted streets until I found a taxi to take me back to my hotel.

I returned the next day, after a night of terrors and nightmares, after half an hour on the phone convincing the people who had contracted me that jet lag had left me with an impossible headache.

The port of La Boca was cold and foggy with the solitary, mean look peculiar to ports that have been condemned to a slow death.

A few tourists wandered, looking lost, past the false cheer of the painted houses; the cold was damp, insidious, tenacious.

Not knowing how I'd got there, I found myself in a museum I'd visited on other trips, an uncommonly sad museum, deserted, with large and poorly lit galleries, its walls painted in unlikely colours — bilious green, dirty yellow, faded blue — and covered with paintings from every style and every era, in an incomprehensible cacophony, as if they had been relegated there all the better to be forgotten.

With the vague idea that, seeing as I was already there, I might as well head up to the third floor and take another look at Quinquela's paintings, the brazenness that matched the tango so well; with the anguish I was feeling, with the stench of death that hung over La Boca, I crossed an enormous gallery, empty of visitors, where the brushing of my footsteps against the floor created a whisper of echoes.

And then I saw her. At the far end of the gallery, to the left, between a horrid landscape of the pampas and an incongruous scene of ladies in mantillas and gentlemen in top hats leaving High Mass, there she was, looking at me from the obscure depths of an oil painting framed in heavy, gilded wood. Her eyes shone as they had at the milonga, half closed in pleasure, as if she were listening to the beat of a tango that was being played only for her in the solitude of that dusty museum; her intensely red lips were gently curled, as they had been then, into a slight smile that was both pained and provocative; her black hair was pulled back in a tall chignon and held in place with a tortoiseshell comb. In the cut of her dress, held in place by a black silk corset, a rosebud stood out, red and barely beginning to open, against her pale skin. A variety of hothouse rose that did not yet exist when her portrait was painted.

The small medallion on the frame, right below the spot where her hands — the same hands that had rested on my shoulder and held my own hand — were clasped at her waist, read: *"Tango is a whispered cry*. Unknown artist. Ca. 1920."

TWO

There were two days to go until my wedding day, three days until my birthday. That was how I had planned it. I loved the idea of being a wife already on the day I turned twenty, and of being able to say for the rest of my life that I had married at the age of nineteen. In the month of January. In the middle of summer.

I still wasn't used to everything being all topsy-turvy, to sweltering in the heat when it was supposed to be cold, to being so poor all of a sudden, to being surrounded by people from so many different countries, so many of whom still spoke Spanish badly.

We had come to Argentina two years earlier, just Papá and I. And thanks to El Rojo — Berstein, that is, my future husband — we had moved into a house in La Boca. Papá spent the few savings we had managed to keep with us from Spain on opening a small carpenter's shop, where he also made shoemakers' lasts, his actual profession.

My grandfather had owned a factory in Valencia that made

shoemakers' lasts. Papá managed it for a few years, until my grandfather died and my uncles burned through the inheritance in a matter of months and left us out on the street. Then Papá, who had already been a widower for years, decided to leave Valencia, where there was no longer anything to keep him but Mamá's grave, and set off for Argentina.

It hadn't been easy for me. I had been raised in a tiny village near Vitoria with a Basque father and a Valencian mother. I had to move to Valencia when I was eight, after Grandmother Begoña died and Grandfather Francesc set aside all the quarrels that had separated him from his daughter and offered my father a job at the factory. And then again, at the age of seventeen, I had to bid farewell to the world that I had built for myself and follow my father to Buenos Aires.

At first I planned to stay in Valencia, but that would have meant living with my aunts and uncles and silly cousins, or else getting married within a couple of months to one of the little swells who kept trying to court me and who, though I had never much liked any of them, I had liked even less since the factory had sunk into ruin, because they were suddenly acting as though they would be doing me a big favour if they were to lead me to the altar.

So I came with him, to start over one more time.

Then El Rojo. That was one of those things one would never have done if one had thought it through first. But I caught his eye, I was the right age for getting married, we owed him so much, he was a good man, and Papá, who was in poor health, had given him his word, because he was panicked by the thought of dying and leaving me all alone so far from home.

And to tell the truth, when I was running to the grocer's on an errand on that January morning, with its infernal heat and the pungent, humid odour rising from the river, I felt happy. Like every girl my age, it thrilled me to think about my wedding, about the bulging trousseau that was stored away in the good trunk, about the wedding dress hanging in the mirrored wardrobe that we had brought from Valencia, about the idea that I would be called *señora*, about the party we'd throw for the few friends we had here, and about — well, every wedding has its groom.

Mine was tall and stout and wore a beard, a moustache, and long, reddish-blond hair. He was fifteen years older than me, a boatswain on a freighter, and German, though he spoke Spanish very well. He was a real man, not like those spoiled little pale, perfumed, cravated Valencian toffs who used to escort us from High Mass when my aunt and cousins and I rode along the Alameda and down Viveros in the chaise.

I had never seen El Rojo wear a cravat. When he visited me on the Sundays he wasn't off at sea, he would wear a black silk ribbon necktie that fell to the middle of his chest and a tight linen jacket that wrinkled the moment he sat down and turned damp under his arms.

At first we scarcely spoke, but later on, bit by bit, while I worked on my embroidery — my father forbade me to darn or mend things in front of visitors — and the two of them sipped the maté that we had all come to love, he began to tell us stories about his voyages, about what he had seen in distant countries, the dangers he had faced, the colours of the sea and sky when you are in the middle of the ocean and don't know if you will ever reach dry land.

"Sometimes you start to see things that aren't there," he would say. "Not just you, everybody. Somebody'll say, 'Look, look, an island,' and before you know it everybody sees it. And then it turns out it was a cloud that melts away a minute later. Sometimes, out at sea, I wonder whether all this" — and he would make a little gesture with his hands, as if to embrace not only our modest sitting room but the whole district, and who knows, maybe all Buenos Aires — "whether all this isn't just a dream too, a mirage that keeps me going and that I myself have just made up. Whether you, Miss Natalia," he went on with unexpected timidity, "aren't just a story I tell myself, like the story of the sirens that others tell. But that only happens to me sometimes, when the voyage gets long. I think that once you are my wife, Miss Natalia, it won't happen to me any more."

I thought it odd that a grown man like El Rojo, as big and strong as he was, would get such ideas into his head, but when I recalled our own crossing from Spain I could imagine that on the high seas you might think things that you would never have thought in your own home, on land, where the ground doesn't swell and the walls don't sway and the view out of the window never changes.

But we had few such afternoons, because, even though Rojo tried to arrange short voyages during the period of our engagement, there were times when we did not see one another for weeks on end and I could even go out on a stroll with some Italian girlfriends who lived nearby and also had seafaring fiancés. We couldn't go dancing, though that was what we loved best, because it wasn't decent to go out dancing when you were betrothed; nor could we go to the cinema hall, because it was too expensive and too dark; but we would get together to sew and chat, or to walk about and listen to the music that filtered out of the cafés, the music of the tango, for which we were all mad.

I remember the first time I heard it. Just one song. I was fifteen, at the ball in the Teatro Principal in Valencia, wearing a pale pink dress and holding an ivory fan that had belonged to my mother. I heard that music there, and all at once I felt as if all my bones had gone soft.

A short, very dark man, costumed with a poncho, spurs, and high-heeled boots, played a kind of accordion that was almost larger than he was, accompanying a couple who danced alone on the dance floor under the astonished gazes of the best Valencian society. One passionate song. A dance of closed eyes and shadows and tobacco smoke in that huge theatre of marble columns and crystal chandeliers. One woman, swaying like a flower in the wind, and one man with the proud bearing of a bullfighter, lifting her, cleaving to her as if bound by a curse.

After that song, the little swell accompanying me took me immediately to the confectioner's shop to have refreshments while he apologized for the spectacle I had just witnessed. That night my dreams were filled with the rhythms of the tango, and when Papá broached the subject of Argentina, the first thing I thought was: "That's where they dance the tango," and I told him I would go.

Later came Rojo and the afternoons spent embroidering in the sitting room and waiting to get married so that I could go out to dance in some café.

I had been taught the tango by María Esther, a girl my own age who was born in Buenos Aires. She was the daughter of the book-keeper for an important shipping company, and they had a Victrola at home. We often got together there, just us girls, to practise dancing with each other, dying of laughter when we had to play the man's role, imagining with our eyes closed that we were in the grip of impossible passions like the ones you read about in serialized stories in the Sunday papers. We'd talk about fiancés and trousseaus, drink maté and, taking turns to crank the Victrola, play gramophone records over and over again that made us feel all pins and needles without our understanding why, as if tiny burning insects were crawling through our veins.

"And you, do you love El Rojo?" María Esther asked me one day when it was just the two of us alone. She was betrothed to a rich farmer she scarcely ever saw, so rarely did he come to Buenos Aires.

"He's my fiancé," I recall answering her, almost feeling offended, because for the moment I couldn't think of anything else to say. "Do you love Luis Alfonso?"

She broke out laughing. "He's my fiancé!" She tossed my own answer back at me.

Then we both had a good laugh. Afterwards a silence fell, until my friend finally broke it. "You know what, Natalia? Mamá says that men *do*, and women *are*. Okay, so you and I *are*."

"I don't understand what you mean."

"Men work, move around, come and go, play, drink, some of them kill. They shave in the morning, so they scrape off the skin they had the day before. That way they don't grow, they're always new, get it? But we just *are*. Girls, mothers, wives. We're sweet, polite, faithful, good. We grow, we become. They'll ask a man, 'What do you *do, compadre?*' Us, they ask, 'What *are* you, a missus or a miss?' Get it?"

I didn't laugh this time because it wasn't funny any more. I had never thought of it that way, but funny it was not.

"When you get married to El Rojo, you'll be his wife, and I'll be Luis Alfonso's. Nobody will ever ask us, 'What do you do, ma'am?' because everybody already knows what."

"But that's a good thing, isn't it?"

María Esther shrugged her shoulders and brewed some more

maté. "Wouldn't you like to dance the tango in a theatre and hear the applause and have men look at you with desire and bring you flowers?"

"I don't know. I don't think so."

But that was a lie, because when María Esther screwed up her eyes and looked at me closely while asking her question, I could hear the tango in my head and I knew that, yes, I would love it; but I also knew that it could never be, and that after I got married to Rojo I would only dance now and again at parties with him, when he was home from his ship, and only until our children arrived at that — and they would arrive, because that's why one got married.

"It wouldn't be decent," I added.

"No. Definitely not decent," she said with a mischievous smile, offering me a cigarette from her father's case.

She ran to shut the sitting-room door and we took refuge behind the green velvet curtains, keeping the windows half-open so we could toss out the stubs if anybody walked in.

"So why are you telling me all this?" I asked.

"I don't really know, Natalia. It must be because I'm afraid of getting married and having to move so far away, out to the pampas, and be stuck there for ever with Luis Alfonso. I . . ." She took a deep drag of her cigarette and stared out at the water of the port, already turning the amethyst colour that announces nightfall. "I don't know whether I love him, get it? I like seeing him, I like it when he takes me to the theatre, and I don't mind it if he grabs me when Mamá isn't looking." She paused again, avoiding my eyes. "We've even kissed a couple of times, and, well, it wasn't bad. But I've read how you're supposed to feel when you're in love and — that's not what's happened to me, kid. That's all."

She carefully stubbed out the cigarette on the window sill and tossed it almost angrily into the street. I threw out mine as well and put my hand on her shoulder. "That isn't really so, María Esther."

"Of course it's true."

"No, I mean the things you've read. That's just literature, lies that writers have made up."

She stubbornly shook her head. "When I was fifteen, there was a maid we had that Mamá had to fire, because, well, you know . . ."

I quickly nodded, not wanting her to think I was stupid.

"She told me about what you feel when your man touches you, when he just looks at you and it's like liquid fire is drenching you and trickling down inside you, like wild horses are dragging you and you can't stop them." She sighed deeply. "That's what I want to feel, Natalia, just once, before I get married," she said firmly, turning her defiant face towards me.

Before I could answer, Doña Melina came in to light the oil lamps and we had to drop the subject, but from that day on I avoided being alone with her because I knew that her next question was going to be: "And you, Natalia? Wouldn't you like that?"

María Esther got married in the spring, in November, and afterwards we only wrote to each other, but she had promised to come to my wedding and I was burning to ask her, now that she was a married woman, whether she still dreamed about dancing in the theatre or experiencing the book kind of love that's like fire running through your veins.

I had spent a lot of time thinking it over since then, every night when I retired to my single's bed (now that I was about to get married, I always thought of it as a single's bed), and I imagined Berstein in his nightshirt sprawled next to me in bed and knew that this was not it, even though the serialized stories that writers make up never mentioned this, nor did my father, who hadn't explained to me what was supposed to happen when Rojo and I were left alone at home after the wedding.

I don't know whether I would have had the courage to ask my mother, but asking my father was impossible. Despite all the horrible tales that I had heard told about what happened on one's wedding night, I knew that my father would never allow anything bad to happen to me and that, if all the married women I knew had survived it, so would I.

And now that it was just two days away, now that the wedding dress was hanging in my wardrobe — white, with a veil, because my father had decided to spend whatever it took on his only daughter's wedding — I continued to think about it, but from a sort of distance, as if it were somebody else thinking about it, while I was dreaming about the ceremony and the bouquet and, most of all, about the ball afterwards, which my girlfriends and their fiancés would attend, as many of them as were on dry land, and also my father's associates; a ball where the bandoneón would play, and where for the first time I'd give myself over to its magic in the arms of a man. The arms of Berstein. Of Rojo. Of my husband.

That is what I was thinking about when I entered the grocer's shop belonging to Uxío, a Gallego who had spent half his life in La Boca. My father had sent me to the shop for a bottle of Spanish wine that he wished to set aside for a drink with his new son-in-law when the time came.

The sunlight was so bright outside that I could only see shadows when I entered. There was a strong smell of wine and sawdust, a smell of single men, which, for all that, brought to mind fond memories of the tavern on Quart street where I used to go with Amparo as a young girl to buy the red wine that Grandfather Francesc loved.

Suddenly from the dark depths of the rambling shop came the unexpected rending wail of a bandoneón. Still half blinded, I turned like a compass needle towards the sound, leaning my hand on the zinc counter to steady myself, and I involuntarily noticed that four men playing cards at a table next to the billiards had turned to gaze at me, while a skinny boy against the wall played the squeezebox.

My stomach leaped into my chest. A young man, his hat pushed back on his head of black hair, wearing a collarless white shirt and braces, stared at me as if I were an apparition.

"Here for Don Joaquín's wine, dearie?" Don Uxío's voice boomed behind my back.

I nodded yes, unable to take my eyes off the man who had stood up holding his cards in his hand.

Everything turned red. His stare, meeting mine, was like a needle tattooing my heart.

And suddenly this was it: the liquid fire, the powder exploding in my veins, the red-hot iron branding me for ever. This was it, María Esther.

When the grocer handed me the bottle refilled with wine, my hands trembled so that I didn't dare touch it, and I had to draw my handkerchief from my sleeve and wipe my brow.

"Damn this heat!" Uxío exclaimed. "Have a bit to drink, sweet."

He set a small glass of cane liquor down next to me and, without thinking, I, who had never before drunk more than a sip of sweet wine, tossed it down in one gulp.

It burned, like his eyes.

I picked up the bottle and walked to the door, not looking back. I heard someone say, "Diego, kid, what's up with you?" And, refusing to turn back in, I walked out of the shop into the light, into the heat.

There were two days to go until my wedding day, three days until my birthday.

"Fine-looking kid, isn't she?" said the Gallego, setting the bottle of cane liquor down on the table.

Murmurs of agreement. It was all I could do to pry my eyes from the door through which she had gone out. I sat back down, distractedly showing my cards.

"Hey, kid, what're you doing?" said Flaco Martínez, looking crestfallen at the hand I had been dealt.

Paying him no mind, I poured myself a drink and slammed it back.

"Her name's Natalia," the Gallego explained. "She's Don Joaquín Irati's daughter — Basque fellow who came over from Valencia a couple years back."

"She's a fine girl," De Bassi agreed.

"Give her a few years and she'll be a real woman, soon as she learns what a man is. And fills out a little," insisted the shopkeeper, who liked his women big, buxom and wide-hipped.

"There won't be any shortage of candidates," added Canaro.

"She'll be getting married on Sunday. To Berstein. To El Rojo."

"Goddam krauts!" said De Bassi, who followed the war news from Europe and took the Allies' side. "They're even beating us at that."

"El Rojo never gets mixed up in politics. He might still speak Spanish like he's holding an almond under his tongue, but he's as Argentinian as the best of us."

"I couldn't sleep if I was off at sea and left a peach like her at home," said Canaro with a wink. "Buenos Aires is full of lonely men."

Guffaws all around. Without thinking I got up and, as I was on my feet, walked off in the direction of the lavatory in the courtyard. Anything not to keep hearing their comments.

The girl had plucked a string that I didn't know I had inside me. Suddenly every lyric of every tango I had ever danced in every café in Buenos Aires sounded to me like a page from a diary that I had still to write.

I leaned against a wall, took a deep breath, rolled a cigarette, and tried to recall every detail I had seen of her: silhouetted against the light, the glint of a tiny earring, a dark curl peeking out from her chignon, the sleeves of her white blouse transparent in the light that streamed in from outdoors, diminutive feet in a small pair of boots revealing her fine ankles, the ankles of a ballerina . . . That was it.

But even so . . . Even so, I panted as if from heavy lifting, cigarette trembling in my jittery hands, and my stomach churned when I recalled the Gallego's words: "She'll be getting married on Sunday."

She had been living in La Boca for two years and it was only now when it was too late that I'd met her. I had no idea who this El Rojo was, but I was sure that, whoever he might be, he didn't deserve her. From what Canaro said, he had to be a sailor, a guy who'd leave her alone for weeks and months at a time, struggling on her own to make ends meet in La Boca, a district brimming with whores and *compadritos*. Honest fellows, too, but fellows who happened to be lonely, no wives, no family, nobody to lean on, far from home.

The Gallego's courtyard was a jumble of empty bottles, rusting cans and discarded rubbish, but a slender tree had sprouted by the back wall, and overhead the sky was clear, wide and blue, with a scattering of frayed clouds lit bright by the midday sun. More or less like my life. Underfoot, the filth from which I had emerged — the squalid tenement house on Corrientes where my parents lived after they came over from Genoa, the poverty that was all I had seen throughout my childhood, the long years of factory work, of night-times studying by oil lamp so I might climb out of it all someday. Overhead, the open sky, the world I had always dreamed of, which day by day seemed to move further off but to shine all the brighter. And here in the middle, today's grind, the newspaper I worked at, changing my name from Giacomo to Diego (sounds better for a tanguero), my bachelor flat, the tango I danced every night in the best cafés. My friends were all musicians, instrumentalists, singers, composers, songwriters — or dancers, like me.

But it wasn't enough. And though I had always known that it wasn't enough, in one instant the girl had made me understand that the sky was still clear — far away, but clear, for anyone who had the will to fly.

For that alone, she deserved a present, so I walked back in and proposed, "We could play at her wedding."

"What wedding?" asked Flaco Martínez, who never noticed what was going on but was a tolerably good piano player.

"The girl's. Natalia's."

"They already signed up Firpo's orchestra," said the Gallego from behind the bar.

"Of course they did," Canaro smiled. "They want the clodhoppers who can't follow our beat to be able to dance. But they must have some cash if they could hire Firpo."

Firpo and Canaro were night and day, especially in the rhythms they used, and a rivalry was slowly but surely growing between them. We professionals danced "à la Canaro"; everyone else, "à la Firpo".

"What if you went and serenaded the doll on Saturday night?" the Gallego suggested. "That's what girls in Spain love best of all."

I glanced around at everyone there.

"Who's game?"

"Count on my violin," said Canaro. "Right about midnight, during our break at the Royal."

"You coming, Yuyo? No squeezebox, no tango," I said, knowing that Yuyo would play awake or asleep, paid or unpaid.

"You bet!"

"Flaco?"

"Not with the piano . . ."

"But you can also play flute."

"Bring your guitar and I'll give the flute a whirl," he answered.

"How about second fiddle?" asked De Bassi.

By now we were all smiling, as if all of a sudden playing music, the way we earned our bread, was some kind of mischievous prank.

"Do you know where the kid lives, Gallego?"

"On Necochea, in a one-storey house, painted blue."

"OK then, gents. Tomorrow, midnight, at the Royal. We'll leave together from there. I'll be dancing at La Marina — I'll catch up with you during the break."

I draped my coat over my shoulder and walked out, though I didn't need to be at the newspaper office until later that afternoon. Letting my feet wander, I found myself standing on Necochea street in front of a blue house where I hadn't lost anything. Except, perhaps, a bit of my heart.

I arrived at our house dizzy from the heat, and from something else that I had no word for, that I wished to have no word for. The cool air in the entrance hall felt like my mother's hand on a feverish night, and I couldn't help my eyes filling with tears at the thought of her, of how she had left me so alone, so young, right when a girl needs someone to talk to. I didn't even have the comfort of going to see María Esther and telling her what had happened to me at the grocer's, just as she couldn't tell me what had happened to her after her wedding when everyone left her alone with the fellow who had just become her husband.

My loneliness weighed on me like a marble tombstone, so I headed towards the sitting room, where I thought I could hear a rumbling of voices, in search of company that would pull my thoughts in a different direction.

The door was ajar, and from the hallway I could see the tip of a man's boot — El Rojo's boot.

I stood stock-still, holding my breath without knowing why,

and, squatting to set the bottle on the floor, pulled out a kerchief to dry the sweat that streamed down my face.

"So now you know how things stand," my father was saying. "I had to let you know; I hope you understand. Natalia is all I have in the world, and even though I know I am leaving her in good hands, I wanted to be frank with you, in case you'd rather back out."

My breath was taken away. I didn't know what my father had been talking about, but here he was giving Rojo a chance to undo the wedding. It felt almost as if someone had just knocked over a house of cards, but at the same time as if a very bright light was being shone into some very dark corner.

"I'm a man of my word, Don Joaquín," Berstein was now replying. "As you know. I will care for Natalia with all my strength, this I swear to you. I love her. I have always loved her, from the first time I saw her, when she was still a child. You will not regret giving her to me."

"Treat her well, son. Natalia, despite the state you see her in here, is a young lady. She deserved better than I've been able to give her, but, first, I married her mother against the will of her whole family, who wanted something else for her, and took her away to a village in Vitoria where the poor dear was consumed by sorrow and poverty; and then, after her father forgave her and I swallowed my pride and we returned to Valencia, she barely survived two more years. Natalia lived like a queen for a short time, and now she is suffering hardships again, as in her childhood."

"You both live honourably, Don Joaquín. This is no tenement, and Natalia has no need to work outside the house."

"As you know, this house is all I own; the only thing I can leave her."

"I earn good money. We will do well. I am going to treat her like a queen, I promise you this."

Silence followed. I didn't know whether to take advantage of it and make a bit of noise, as if I were just coming back from the shop.

"Treat her well the day after tomorrow, son. Natalia is an innocent young woman. She knows nothing about men."

"I swear to you I will, Don Joaquín. Everything will happen slowly, at its own rhythm."

"Thank you, son. I wish I could have talked to her about it, but with a daughter, such things — it isn't the same as if she were a boy; you understand what I'm saying. That's why I'm telling you all this."

"And where is she now?"

"She went out for a moment to Uxío's shop. She'll be back at any time."

I picked up the bottle and tiptoed into the kitchen, where I set about clattering with the dishes so that they'd think I had gone there directly to change the water the chickpeas were soaking in for our evening stew. In fact, all I had left to make for lunch was the rice.

If I had heard what my father told Rojo earlier that day, before

I had gone out and come back, maybe things would have turned out differently. But he had sent me to the shop so that he could talk with Rojo in private, and that changed everything, because there I had run into someone's gaze, a gaze that was all it took to knock down the world I had barely begun to build for myself.

I left the editorial room just before nine. I had planned to drop by my flat first, but I saw that I wouldn't make it. I had picked up my tango outfit before going to the newspaper office, so I decided to grab a bite at La Fonda de los Artistas on Corrientes and then walk over to Salta and Rivadavia, where I'd be dancing that night at Café La Puñalada.

The hours I had spent at the office had kept my mind busy, but now, walking out into the warm January night and mingling with the crowds in the city centre streets, I felt all at once as if my heart would break from loneliness, as if I had suddenly grown aware that my life made no difference to anyone. My parents had died years earlier in a yellow fever epidemic, my brothers and sisters had scattered to the four winds, nobody in Genoa could possibly remember my family any more, and even in Buenos Aires, the city where I had grown up, I didn't know anyone but the boys at the newspaper and cafés. And Grisela. She was only my dancing partner, though she'd have liked to be more. But I had never wanted to tie myself to anyone. Never wanted to fall into the same trap as so many other immigrants — having lots of kids, then climbing one rung at a time down the ladder of poverty. Like my parents.

I didn't have a tango singer's voice, and I wasn't good enough at playing an instrument, though I could handle the guitar passably well. I would never gain fame and fortune through music. The newspaper and dancing the tango provided me with enough to survive and cover my modest luxuries, but not enough to support a wife and start a family. Besides, frankly speaking, I had never "loved a chick till betrayal, till madness, till death", as the tango songs were starting to put it. The only girlfriends I'd ever had were poor girls prematurely aged by factory work, the misery of life in the tenements, dreams too soon shattered, the brutality of their fathers, their brothers, and later their husbands; girls who had once been flowers, and who ended up withered and trodden underfoot.

La Fonda was crowded to bursting, as always, but Doña Clemencia set up a table for me by the kitchen and served me a stew with more potatoes than meat and a glass of red wine. After, I rolled a cigarette and smoked it outside. I felt sweat streaming down my flanks as I walked towards the café where Grisela would be waiting impatiently for me in her tight skirt and high heels, staring into the green bottom of the glass of absinthe that rarely strayed from her hands those days.

The grandiose façades of the houses kept reminding me how I had sworn to myself a few years earlier that I'd be in Paris by

1920, leaving behind provincial Buenos Aires to undertake my conquest of the true capital of the world. But back then I was barely twenty years old, and with my hopes raised by the success of the first tango dancers in Europe I had conceived the notion that everything was possible. Now, walking up Rivadavia past Café Tortoni, I was starting to feel like an old man watching his youth slip away before him, knowing that he will never catch up with it.

She would be getting married on Sunday. Tomorrow night, I might catch sight of her at her balcony. And then, never again. Card games, dancing in cafés, articles for *La Nación*, the emptiness of knowing that this is all there is; you got dealt a bad hand, kid, whatcha gonna do?

I stubbed out my cigarette fiercely and, putting on my best imitation of a *compadrito*, entered La Puñalada, thinking that the café's name — the Knife Stab — was well chosen. I found Grisela leaning against the bar with her absinthe. The dance floor, as on every Friday, was full of couples. And single men with hungry stares.

I laid my hand on her shoulder. She turned to look at me with frightened eyes.

"Oh! It's you, Diego."

"Just got here. I'm going to go change."

She nodded and went back to staring vacantly at the mirror before her. There was a bruise on her arm, right above the elbow, poorly hidden by the black gauze sleeve of her dancing dress. I didn't mention it.

We left just past midnight. She wouldn't let me walk with her, because some rich guy had promised to drive her home in his car. I gazed into her eyes, searching for something that wasn't there: contempt, fear, hope, defiance, anything. They were glazed over, like a window in the middle of winter.

I ran my thumb across her cheek. She flashed a flat, absent smile at me.

"Tomorrow at La Marina. Remember, kid."

She agreed without a word. I walked out into the empty street, feeling a vague desire to stab someone.

After a long night of tossing and sweating, I awoke to the thought: *Tomorrow I'm getting married.* Suddenly I felt like a half-dead insect caught in a swirling storm drain, just before the darkness closes in. I shut my eyes tight, said an Ave Maria as my mother had taught me to do when I needed to calm down, pulled the sheets around myself, and wished with all my might that I would keep sleeping for years and years so that tomorrow would never come, so that El Rojo would have time to find himself some other bride and have five children before I awoke.

María Esther's mother, Doña Melina, had come by the afternoon before to tell me that my friend wasn't going to be able to come to my wedding. She was pregnant and suffering from occasional bleeding — normal in the first few months, but bad enough for such an uncomfortable journey to be inadvisable. I couldn't keep my eyes from welling with tears at the thought. I wouldn't even have the consolation of talking with her woman to woman, as I had so often before we were married; she would not be there to help me into my dress, as I had helped her; I'd have to put up with the Italian girls, who had been hoping to take part in a real wedding while they still waited for weddings of their own.

Doña Melina must have noticed what was going through my head, because she hugged me like a daughter and offered to be the one who helped me get ready for the church. But I told her it wasn't necessary and that I was sure that Gina, Beatrice and Vanina would be delighted to lend me a hand.

"It's normal for you to be restless," she told me, right before she left. "This is a huge step, dear, but it's one you have to take. Your fiancé is a good man who loves and respects you, and that's the most important thing. If you didn't have him, when your father passes you'll be easy prey for any *compadrito*, like so many girls we both know. Or you'd turn into an old maid, from home to church and back, up all night surviving on whatever miserable piecework you could get, so they could pay you half of what a man makes for the same work. Maybe some day things will change, like they say in the Feminist Union, but for the time being a woman needs a husband, Natalia."

"And do you think," I dared ask when we were nearly at the door, "that it's true what they say, that love will come with time?"

She smiled and seemed to stare off at something far away that I couldn't see.

"Sometimes. When both sides put in their bit. If they don't lose their respect for each other, if they work for a future that they both want to achieve. Look, dear," she said, taking my arm and putting her mouth up to my ear, as if she feared someone might hear, though we were alone in the house, "I'm going to give you a piece of advice, because I know you don't have anyone else who'll tell you: let your husband know how things stand from the first day; tell him what you like and what you don't like; don't let him think he has a right to do anything just because he's a man. Tell him softly, of course, sweetly, and never in front of others, because one thing a man can't bear is to hear people start telling him that his wife wears the trousers in his house, but don't let him step all over you." She waved her hand to cut off what I wanted to say. "I'm sure this isn't what you've been hearing up to now, but we aren't living in our grandmothers' times, and I want you to be happy, Natalia. When a woman isn't happy, she turns bitter, and then she embitters everything she touches — her children, her husband, her neighbours. Get as much out of life as it has to give, however little that might be. And remember, you have things that other people would give an arm and a leg for. Don't think about what you're losing, think about what you stand to gain, my dear. Come, give me a kiss."

We hugged again in the shadowy entrance way.

"Come and see me whenever you want. Ever since María Esther left, I only have men at home, and I'm all alone too."

That conversation kept going through my head, even after I went to bed, and when I got up I felt confused and frightened.

Doña Melina was right — what she told me was not what I had been taught as a child, not what I had heard from my aunts, my cousins, the maids. She had meant well to tell me, but I would almost have rather heard the usual story: that one must be resigned, make sacrifices, put on a good face, and serve God, one's parents, one's husband, one's children — serve, always serve, because that was what we women were created to do. And the women who don't do so are bad.

I walked around the house in my nightgown, making sure everything was clean and neat, because I wanted to devote the day before the wedding to getting myself ready, and that meant everything else had to be done first. But luckily I had been smart about it, and for the past two weeks had been doing all the chores that needed finishing so that I'd have plenty of time to bathe, wash my hair and do my nails.

My father would be in the workshop until evening, as always. Today he wouldn't even come home for lunch, leaving me to take my bath in the courtyard. I put the big pot to heat on the stove so I could fill the washtub with lukewarm water, and I started bringing out all the things I'd need: the good towel, the perfumed soap we'd brought from Valencia, the cologne, the brilliantine, and the Nievina cream that today I would spread not only on my face but all over my body. My stomach tightened at the thought that someone else's hands would soon be touching my body. Big hands. A man's hands. Rojo's rough sailor hands, as big as baker's shovels, callused all over from struggling with the ship's cables.

Berstein hadn't even kissed me yet. When I pictured his moustache pressed against my mouth, it made me slightly queasy — not quite nauseous, but enough to set my hands to trembling. Of course, that was probably because I had never tried it; maybe I'd like it, as the Italian girls said about themselves and their fiancés.

It was as hot as blazes, and it hadn't even rung nine yet. The plants in the courtyard were drooping. Even the little tree at the back, the one that put out yellow flowers in spring and whose name I didn't know, looked half dead. Only the geraniums and the carnations remained defiantly crimson, and the climbing bellflowers continued spreading like a flood across the garden wall that separated our house from the neighbour's. I fetched two pails of water from the tank and watered them all, so as not to feel their envious stares while they watched me bathe. The sky was a perfect blue, without a cloud, as if it had been painted, and already the smell of jasmine was strong enough to make your head spin.

I filled the tub — half hot water, half cold, to avoid a shock — then undressed, after looking in every direction to be sure no-one was spying on me, and slipped into the water with a sigh. It felt so good it seemed a sin, but I knew that it was all right, that every girl has a right to enjoy her last bath before she's married, even if it had to be like this, in a foreign land, without her mother, without a girlfriend to talk to, without any feeling of liquid fire from the man who would soon be her husband and all but her master.

Against my will I began to think about the man from the day before, at Uxío's. I remembered most of all his gaze, though I couldn't have told you what colour his eyes were; the tension of his lean body; his long, fine fingers holding aloft a fan of cards. They had called him Diego.

I lathered all over with soap, trying to change my train of thought: the wedding dress was ironed; the stockings wrapped in tissue; the shoes in the box; the veil pinned to the garland of wax orange blossoms. Papá would pick up the bouquet on his way home from work, and at night he would give me Mamá's good earrings, the ones he had been saving for my wedding, which I could hardly remember because she had only worn them on important occasions.

It crossed my mind that it would have been nice if we could have arranged for the portrait. That had been an idea of Papá's, soon after we arrived in La Boca. Although it sort of embarrassed me at the time, now I was thinking that it would have been nice. Papá had heard of an artist, a fellow named Nicanor Urías, who people said was a magnificent portrait painter, and Papá had got the notion into his head of commissioning him to paint my picture so that my children would always have something to remember their mother by. He never mentioned it, but I always knew how much it pained him not to have so much as a photograph of his own wife, and sometimes I also thought that, with all the money my uncles had squandered in Valencia, we might have commissioned one of my mother when she was young and beautiful, before the illness that finally killed her had aged her prematurely. It could have been hanging in our sitting room right now, and I could have looked at her whenever I was alone in the house, and from her eyes, so sweet, so cheerful, felt that she was still watching over me.

But like my mother's portrait, mine was not to be. Papá told me that Urías' prices were too high and, now that we had to lay on the wedding, we couldn't afford any more expenses. But the Italian girls told me that the problem wasn't the money; it was that the artist had a bad reputation. People said he was a bit of a sorcerer, because his mother was a Brazilian witch, and they said his portraits looked so good and so lifelike because when he painted them, he imbued them with a bit of the soul of the person he was painting.

I found this impossible to believe, and I was very surprised that my father, such a religious and serious man, would think that there could be any truth in it at all. Perhaps it was simply that the painter was a mulatto and Papá preferred not to deal with coloured people. Or maybe it was really about the money, because he also went to speak with another artist, someone named Quinquela Martín, who was painting portraits of people in the district for an exhibition he was putting together, and he came back saying the same thing, that for the time being we had to think about the wedding preparations, and that later on we would see.

I don't know why, but that day, while I was getting ready, all I could think about were things that could never be, while the things that really were possible, that were necessarily going to happen, slipped like soap through my fingers.

I washed my hair carefully, rinsed it out with a bit of vinegar to bring out the shine, and let it lie loose on my back to dry while I combed it. Then I put on the cream, skipping my back because I didn't want my hair to get greasy again, and opened the violet cologne, which reminded me of my mother and of Valencia.

It was only then that I remembered I would have to spend the rest of the day in the kitchen baking the tarts, fairy cakes and rolls. I burst out laughing at the image of how sweaty I'd be all over again by nightfall, after hours at the oven. But at least my hair would be clean, and I could always take another quick dip in the tub, unless it occurred to my fiancé to come and visit us after supper.

What, I wondered, was he doing just then? Bathing like me, getting ready for his wedding night? Or out with his friends, taking leave of his bachelor life, swilling cane liquor in some tavern? And the other man. What was that man doing while I was here drying my hair in the courtyard?

Feeling foolish and a bit guilty, I started picturing how the day before my wedding might have gone if things had been different — if we had still been living in Valencia, if my mother hadn't died, if I were about to marry a man like the fellow in the shop.

I would have woken up then in a house full of women, listening to the comings and goings of maids while Mamá sipped chocolate with me and talked about all the things that needed to be done. I wouldn't have had to step near the kitchen, for Grandfather would have asked Remedios to take care of all the baking, and someone else would have been in charge of decorating the hall for the party afterwards. We would have gone to the cathedral at mid-morning, to give thanks to God and to watch over the floral arrangements . . .

The church! I had completely forgotten that I needed to go to church at six that afternoon to confess. But, dear Lord, what was I going to confess? That I had enjoyed my bath? That I had wasted time thinking about vain and impossible things? That I was dreaming about the wedding dance and tango music? That I had imagined, though only for a moment, that the hands that would caress me on the day after my wedding might have been those of a man I had seen for scarcely one minute in the shadowy depths of the grocer's shop? Could any of these things be sins?

I kissed the medallion with the image of Our Lady of the Forsaken, patron saint of Valencia, that I had worn around my neck since First Communion, and without giving it another thought I went inside to finish getting everything ready.

I left La Marina wearing my dancing clothes and my hat. My heart was beating at a frenzied pace. I gripped the guitar as if it were about to fly away and gulped at the night air, full of the seaside smells of stagnant water, oil from passing ships, and occasional whiffs of the jasmine and carnations that women grew here and there by the doors of their homes.

I was nearly out of breath when I reached the Royal. There the boys were, smoking languidly and joking around as always. The lights of the café reflected off their pomaded hair, making them look like respectable gentlemen despite the musical instruments they carried and the party atmosphere wafting through the district. They had left their hats inside the Royal and were all wearing suits and bow ties. I noticed for the first time since I met them that I was the only one who didn't wear a stylishly trim moustache. This frivolous detail made me feel different once more, as I had on so many other occasions in life. Different, odd, out of place. The only one for whom this was not a mere Saturday night lark.

We all set off as a gang, debating what kind of programme we should offer, the pros and cons of our favourite songs. I took little part in the discussion. My mind was off in other matters, and everything seemed fine to me so long as I could see her again.

In a matter of minutes we were standing at the door to her house. We started tuning up before anyone had even looked out of the windows. Then Canaro lifted his bow, and we began the set with a lively little waltz that had been very popular the previous winter. A milonga followed, then a tango, the night's first.

By then there were men at all the neighbours' doors applauding when each song ended, and a few women at the windows, half hidden behind the lowered blinds. But Natalia's house remained dark, as if no-one there had noticed the serenade, or as if they had decided not to accept our humble tribute.

I had to dry my hands on my trouser legs after each song. Mumbling in a low voice so that no-one could hear, I repeated her name like a prayer, *Natalia, Natalia, Natalia*, trying to make her get out of bed, come to the window and look at me, though it were for the last time.

By the fifth piece, when our serenade was looking like a town dance and the neighbours had started to make requests — two men had taken to dancing under the street lamp at the corner — my prayers were heard and the door to the house opened. An older man, no doubt Natalia's father, waited until we finished playing. Then, his face almost breaking into a smile that never quite took shape, he asked, "Did El Rojo send you?"

Canaro performed a florid bow and explained that, as we had learned that his daughter was getting married the next day, we had come to offer the young lady a serenade.

The man smiled and went back inside. I kept staring at the upstairs window, determined not to miss Natalia's appearance. When Canaro gave the next signal I came in as best I could, a few measures late, because I didn't even know what we were playing. It turned out to be Contursi's "Percanta que me amuraste", "Lover Girl, You Left Me", a tango that always stirred my deepest emotions, especially after Castriota wrote lyrics and turned it into "Mi noche triste", "My Lonely Night".

She opened the tiny balcony, smiling and embarrassed, wearing a white nightgown with a pink shawl draped over her arms and shoulders. Her father stood behind her, turning me green with envy each time he caressed her head and sank his fingers into the soft hair that cascaded down her back.

Natalia ran her eyes across us all, but from the moment our gazes met they never parted. I played as if entranced, paying no attention to Canaro's lead, remembering nothing of the programme we had put together, following only the voice of the squeezebox and another voice that sang out inside me, cutting me off from the outside world, while she watched me through her eyelashes and chewed her lips just as I did.

I don't remember what the final song was; I know only that a moment came when everything fell silent. Don Joaquín, from the balcony, offered us a glass of muscatel while excusing his daughter, who, given the lateness of the hour and how early she needed to rise the next morning, could not accompany us. I understood the old man. I would not have allowed her to go downstairs either, to stand around in her nightgown, mixing with a bunch of strange musicians on her last night as an unmarried woman. But all the time that I drank and joked with the boys, I could not stop picturing her upstairs, so close, so far away, lying in a bed that must smell of carnations and woman-child, waiting to give herself to a man who was not me. From the entrance I could see the foot of the stairs that led to her floor. I had to dig my nails into my palms to keep from climbing them.

Before we left, Don Joaquín, in an outburst of generosity and gratitude, invited us all to the wedding. "As friends, not as musicians," he specified. I departed thinking that he could not have wounded me more grievously if he had plunged a gaucho dagger into my ribs, yet I would not miss the chance of seeing her again for anything in the world, even though she would be dressed in white, in a church, for another man.

When I reached Uxío's shop to ask him if I could lie down in some corner until next morning, the sky was filled with stars, but they were all screaming, as if they were made of shattered glass, just shards of something that had once been beautiful and was now broken for ever. As if they were splinters driven into the velvet skin of the night.

I left home walking arm in arm with my father. I had on the white satin dress and the orange-blossom garland, the veil pulled down over my eyes, and clutched a small bouquet of lilies that smelled so sweet it made you swoon. The Italian girls went along behind us, making a racket and chirping like sparrows at daybreak. My father walked slowly, conscious of the importance of the occasion, spiffed out and proud as a peacock in his summer suit, best silk tie and finest panama hat, with a lily in his buttonhole, turning right and left to greet all the neighbours who watched from their doors and windows as we paraded past.

Beatrice's brother was waiting for us at the corner with his mandolin, ready to escort us to the church singing all the traditional wedding songs from his home village.

Papá smiled at me and gave a little squeeze to my hand on his arm. Despite everything that happened afterwards, which I could not have even imagined at the time, I will always remember him like that: smiling, proud, happy. Happy after so many setbacks, so many

bitter sorrows. It has all been worth it for this, I remember thinking, and I think it must have been my first thought that morning
because from the moment I opened my eyes I hadn't had time for
anything else, not even for fully comprehending what it was that I
was about to do. The Italian girls had shown up early, before the
first light of dawn, and were sharing a coffee with me in the kitchen
before starting to comb my hair and dress me when Papá ran out
of his room to "make himself presentable". Only later did we realize
with guilty laughter that we should have been fasting before communion, and we finally agreed among ourselves that coffee was,
after all, nothing more than water with a bit of flavouring. But I was
taken aback at not having thought of it, and I couldn't help imagining what Grandmother Begoña would have said if she had found
out: that I was a bad Christian and that it would bring us bad luck.
So I begged Our Lady of the Forsaken for forgiveness and promised to make confession as soon as I could.

The memory of that man's eyes hadn't let me sleep peacefully
all night, and they were still with me, but not fully formed. It was
as if they were inside me, watching the same things I saw: the lilies
in my bouquet, the smiles on the women neighbours, the newly
swept street, the big, dark birds that circled lazily over our heads
and then suddenly took off flying as if in fear from the peeling bells
of the church of San Juan Evangelista.

The entrance of the church was packed. I had no idea so many
people knew us. Or maybe all weddings are like that. The only

wedding I had seen was María Esther's, but she had married in the city, a more exclusive setting. This was La Boca, and everything that happened here was everybody's business.

By the time we reached the entrance my legs were trembling and Papá had to support me for an instant.

"Dizzy?" he asked.

I shook my head and forced myself to smile.

"What's the matter, darling, are you afraid?"

For a moment I couldn't decide whether to tell the truth or to make light of the matter. In the end I nodded yes.

"That's normal, sweet. It'll all be over soon."

I still don't understand how I managed to utter the words, but right there, standing steps away from the crowd that awaited us at the church door, men smoking cigarettes, women waving their fans, I whispered softly to him, "Papá, why didn't you ever ask me if I wanted to marry El Rojo?"

All colour drained instantly from his face. He stared into my eyes and gulped — I know he did, because twice I saw his Adam's apple move up and down, up and down. The aroma of the lilies enveloped us like a warm cloud. Sweat was starting to drip down our temples. Papá raised my veil delicately with one hand, took his handkerchief from his pocket, and wiped my face with it as gently as could be, then dried his own face and put the handkerchief away.

"Don't you want to?" he finally asked.

It was not the time to argue. Everyone was watching us. The

Italian girls, who had gone on ahead, were making signs from the church door as if to hurry us along.

"It isn't that, Papá," I said, more and more flustered. "Yes. Of course I do. Yes, but — I don't know — it would have been nice if someone had asked me."

"Didn't *he* ask you?"

I bit my lips and foolishly shook my head.

"But how was I supposed to know that? Confound it! Nobody ever tells me anything. How was I to imagine that Berstein had asked me for your hand without asking you first?" The perplexity he had felt at first seemed now to be giving way to an irritation that could quickly turn into anger. "But honestly, now, Natalia, don't you love him?"

"I don't know," I dared to say, looking down at my feet.

"Well, that takes the cake! Here I've spent months trying to convince myself that you're not a little girl any more, and now you come out with this."

"It's nothing, Papá," I defended myself. "It must be my nerves."

The church bells — poorly forged, tinny, but wedding bells after all — were still ringing. People were drilling holes in us with their stares. The Italian girls hopped from foot to foot, unable to understand what we were still doing there, facing each other, talking as if it were the most normal thing in the world. And at that moment, Berstein appeared in the door of the church, with a pathetic mien, I thought, like a lost dog in a distant port. He was wearing a natural-coloured pinstripe suit, stiff collar and drooping ribbon necktie; he had washed and combed his red shock of hair, and he was grasping the brim of his hat as if it might fly away like a live bird. I suddenly felt so sorry for this mountain of a man waiting, so humble and so clean, for me, that I flashed him a smile, turned back to Papá, and asked, "How's my lipstick?"

"You've chewed it all off," he answered, also smiling broadly. "Shall we go in?"

"Let's go, Papá."

"Confound it, Natalia, you gave me such a start! I'm too old for shocks like that."

We set off walking slowly, solemnly, receiving people's smiles and congratulations. Berstein went back into the church to await me at the altar, as we had planned. Papá, leaning close to my ear, whispered, "You look beautiful, darling. If only your mother could see you. She would be so proud of you."

My eyes welled with tears and, when the opening strains of the wedding march were played on someone's violin — we had no organ in the church of San Juan in La Boca — I suddenly recalled how my mother had married the man she had chosen herself, twenty-odd years ago, over the objections of her entire family. I understood then two things with utter certainty: that she would not have been proud of me, and that it was too late now to turn back.

The wedding couldn't have seemed longer if I'd been holding my breath underwater the whole time. At first I thought for a moment, standing at the threshold and watching them talk before she entered arm in arm with her father, that something might be going on. Perhaps they had just become aware of some impediment. Perhaps their hasty marriage was being called off. But it must have been nothing, because Don Joaquín simply dried Natalia's face with his handkerchief — she seemed to have been weeping — and they entered the church.

After that, things stayed on course. A mountain of a man, red-headed and smiling like an idiot, waited for her at the altar next to a blond woman in a black mantilla. The four of them knelt. I stood to one side, pressed against a column, so that I might at least watch her profile, silhouetted against her father's.

She seemed startled, like a small animal. The priest sprinkled his Latin phrases over them in the meantime, making the congregation rise and kneel like puppets on strings. It had been many years since I last entered a church. Though I only vaguely recalled what I was supposed to do, I moved my lips in the responses without taking my eyes off her, the only flame that attracted me among all those candles, hoping for a miracle that was not to come. I knew it would not come when the priest, aided by two altar boys, spread a white cloth that covered her head across the man's shoulders. It was a symbol of the wife's subjection to her husband, but it reminded me instead of the sheets that would cover the two of them in bed that very night.

Then came the business of the rings and the "I do"s. The man pronounced his in a loud, decisive voice. She uttered hers like a prayer, like a light breeze whispering among the reeds.

There was nothing else to see. When people started standing up to receive communion, I took my leave of Natalia for ever and fled, planning to get on the first tram that would take me to the centre.

Outside I ran into the boys, who were rolling cigarettes and waiting for the crowd to come out so they could follow them to the hall where the wedding feast would be held. I couldn't slip away unseen, as I had hoped. By the time I realized this the bride and groom were leaving the church, arm in arm, surrounded by a mob of friends congratulating them in several different languages.

My gaze briefly crossed Natalia's, and I felt that she was calling out to me, begging me not to leave her. Perhaps I was mistaken. Perhaps that sudden flash in her eyes had nothing to do with me or my presence, but I made up my mind to drain this cup of poison to the last drop and accompany her as far as I could, so I let the boys drag me along with them, and together we walked for blocks until the music told us where to enter.

The hall was already full of dolls who had beaten us there, waiters standing about with their arms folded, and children running between the legs of adults and hiding under the white cloths of the three tables set out in a U. Canaro greeted Firpo with a nod. The boys on the bandstand smiled at us, recognizing us as colleagues. If it surprised any of them to see their competitors there, they didn't show it.

We drank a few gins while waiting for the couple to arrive and the party to begin. We were already melting in the heat despite the flowering vine that shaded the courtyard. I'd never felt as alone, as lost, as out of place as I did the moment I saw her appear at the door, little more than a white blur against the light. I saw then with burning intensity that it was my destiny to show up too late, or at the wrong time, that it was my destiny to come in second, and that coming in second meant losing, just as surely as if I had come in last.

I put up with the party as best I could, blood pounding in my temples and my stomach tightening with a touch of nausea. She looked at me now and then and quickly averted her gaze, as if it burned.

Waltzes and milongas followed one after the other. The guests ate cakes and pastries and drank cider from Galicia. I smoked, kept quiet and sipped my gin slowly so that I wouldn't look drunk to the happy people all around me.

Then came the first tango. Women squealed. Soon couples were dancing with painstaking cheer under the spreading vine, from light to shade, as if the sun were scattering golden coins over their poor Sunday clothes, turning them into better, nobler garments.

Don Joaquín leaned over Natalia to ask the groom something. The smiling groom shook his head again and again, as if politely declining. Finally the father rose and said a word to the musicians. After they finished playing the tango they took up a waltz. Natalia danced it with her father, under the red-headed German's satisfied gaze. The waltz ended, and she turned to walk to her seat. But Don Joaquín held her back by her hand. Standing in the middle of the dance floor he looked around at everyone and announced, "Ladies and gentlemen, the bride — my daughter Natalia here — has a fancy to dance the tango. I haven't got beyond the waltz and paso doble myself, while the groom, in his own words, has two left feet. Do we have a volunteer in the audience? Is there anyone in this select group who is a good tanguero?"

All eyes converged on me. The boys at my table started saying, almost shouting, that I was the best dancer in Buenos Aires, that I danced in cafés and theatres, and that Natalia couldn't be in better hands.

I stood up straight away. My fingers went to my neck to adjust my scarf, but remembering that I was wearing a bow tie, I straightened my lapels instead. I glided towards them with my best dancer's step, holding out my hand to catch hers, which, despite the heat, felt cold.

Then the world vanished. When she rested her cold hand on my shoulder, when I felt her body against mine, everything disappeared: the noise, the sweaty faces, the smell of a hundred cheap soaps and perfumes, the presence of everything that was still there but not there. All that remained was the music and her body. The tango, her and me.

She danced like a goddess. It was like being tied to a kite held aloft by the evening wind, like flying over fields and streams in a world where time has ceased to exist. I should have died then and there, for I knew that life would never bring me anything to equal this. She would have closed my eyes with her white fingers, and I would have been happy for ever.

But I did not die. The song ended, everyone applauded, and I pulled myself away from her body with a motion that wounded me like a knife stab. I felt around for the nearest table like a blind man. My hand closed on a flower. I offered it to her without a word. It was a carnation, blood-red, that smelled of paradise found and then lost again. She stuck it in her hair, under the orange-blossom garland, without ever taking her shining, feverish eyes off me.

What seemed to me like an eternity must have lasted barely a second, because people were still applauding and calling for us to keep dancing, so we embraced again and danced another song, alone on the dance floor.

Before I could see how it had happened, Canaro was up on the bandstand with his boys. The next tango was one I used to dance with Grisela as a show-stopper. Natalia became a silk handkerchief against my body, a flame enveloping me, a wise flame that understood my movements and burned me a little bit with every step, with every turn. Our breathing grew laboured and I let myself be led into a dark, smooth tunnel from which I could never emerge.

When I separated from her we were both trembling. Sweat streamed over my brows, blinding me. She pulled out a small handkerchief and made as if to dry my forehead, but only held it out without touching me. Then she turned to face the table where her father and her husband applauded. She dropped a graceful curtsy. A group of dolls moved in, surrounding her, hugging her, kissing her enthusiastically.

I had to dance with almost all of them so that no-one would think badly of Natalia. Around mid-afternoon I approached the group where she, her father and the groom sat, to say goodbye and thank them for the invitation.

"Thank you, Don Joaquín," I said, shaking the old man's hand. "Congratulations," I told the German, who offered me his enormous, rough paw. "You've won yourself a pearl, a dancer who'd be the envy of Paris."

The man smiled with satisfaction. "You have made her very

happy with these tangos. I do not know how to dance. Thanks, *compadre*," he replied in the accent of a dog that had learned to speak Spanish. He added in a whisper, squeezing my hand and not taking his eyes off me, "But remember, Natalia has a master now, and the tango is over, understood?"

"Madam," I said, turning to Natalia and feeling as if I were being strangled by the throat and my voice was coming out hoarse, "it has been an honour."

She extended her hand to me, after glancing at her father. I kissed it delicately, like a gentleman.

When I left soon afterwards, her eyes followed me among the guests. I felt those eyes throbbing restlessly behind my back, like thin, hot needles, constantly forcing me to turn towards her. At the door I looked back for the last time. I ran my thumb over my jacket pocket, from which the tip of her handkerchief peered out. I put all my love into that final glance, so that she would know it. I don't think I succeeded.

I had to hold tight to the table's edge to keep from screaming. I bit my lips and suddenly I was sobbing like a fool, crying over some stranger with whom I would have gone to the ends of the earth if he had asked, despite my father, despite my new husband, despite all the women who were smiling at my tears, nodding and whispering among themselves.

"Darling, what's wrong?" Papá asked, holding my hand tenderly. "Are you also thinking of your mother?"

Feeling I was mean, cowardly, base, I nodded, lowering my gaze to keep from meeting his damp eyes.

Doña Melina saved me. She was suddenly behind my seat, squeezing my shoulders and getting me to stand up and accompany her to the ladies' room.

"I'm borrowing her for a moment, Don Joaquín, with your permission. This girl needs a bit of air and some fresh water on her face."

With our arms around each other we entered the house and went into a large bathroom that was so cold compared with the courtyard that a chill passed over me. My girlfriend's mother took off my garland and the carnation that Diego had given me, picked up a towel, wet it in the basin, and without a word began wiping it across my temples, my forehead, and the back of my neck, until I felt better.

"Be careful, Natalia," she whispered quietly into my ear. "That man's dangerous."

"What man?" I asked, feigning innocence because, much as it hurt, I wanted to speak only of him.

Doña Melina stood in front of me, held my chin, and forced me to look at her.

"From now on there cannot be any other man in your life but your husband, do you understand? There's no other way. Your husband, your home, your children when you have them. Be happy with that. Other women have less."

"And him?" I asked in a very low voice, dying of shame.

"He has his own life. Far from you. This is nothing but a passing infatuation, Natalia, what they call a crush. He's a handsome boy and a good dancer. You're an innocent young thing, just hatched from your shell, like María Esther. Give it time and it will heal. Tomorrow everything will be different, you'll see."

"Tomorrow I turn twenty."

I was about to ask her for some advice for the night that would soon begin, when two of the three Italian girls came rushing in to find the bride, and that was the end of the conversation. We left the bathroom together and Doña Melina only had time to whisper, "Come and see me tomorrow if you want to talk."

In the courtyard some married couples were beginning to bid farewell even though it was still light out, and I was there for quite a stretch, shaking hands, kissing sweaty cheeks, being congratulated, feeling the constant presence of Rojo behind my back or at my side, the heat emanating from his enormous body, his hungry eyes craving me as if I were a cake in a bakery window.

"Children," Papá said, coming up behind us and taking us both by the arms, "you can leave whenever you'd like. I'll stay here so long as anyone wants the party to continue, but you two must be tired, and tomorrow is a work day, so if you want to go . . ."

A look of complicity passed between them and Berstein turned to me.

"Shall we go, Natalia?"

I could have said no, but as Rojo didn't dance and we would have to go sooner or later, I agreed without a word and went to find Gina, who had brought a bag with my street clothes so that I wouldn't have to walk through the streets at this hour in my wedding dress.

We started saying goodbye to the guests, going from group to group, laughing at jokes that I didn't understand, thanking people for their presents and good wishes, until, after a long hug from my father, the two of us found ourselves alone in the street. El Rojo, dressed for the wedding in his best summer suit, and I in the matching blue skirt and blouse that I had sewn for myself especially for today.

This was the first time I had been alone with Berstein, really alone, without Papá, without my girlfriends, without anyone else, and I didn't know what to do. He offered me his arm, and so, walking slowly and in silence, we walked towards Necochea, crossing paths with people who were heading for La Boca to have a good time, while my own eyes kept searching in every direction for a hint of his figure, though I knew he would be far away by now, drinking in some dive or playing cards or doing whatever it is that men do when they leave.

We reached home and it struck me as odd that Berstein should be the one taking out the key and opening the door, but now this was his house too, for he had given up the room that he had been renting to use now and then, whenever he was on dry land.

Our bedroom was now going to be the one that had belonged to Papá, who would move into my old room. My girlfriends had insisted on setting it up for my wedding night and refused to let me in to see it before we left for church, so, even though I was in my own house, everything looked odd and different, even the hall, which was the same as ever, dark and a bit sad despite being freshly cleaned.

"A drink?" Rojo proposed, entering the sitting room as if it were the most natural thing in the world. "Yesterday I left a bottle of sweet wine and some pastries here, in case we were hungry."

He poured two glasses without waiting for me to answer, and held out one for me with a nervous smile.

"To our love," he toasted. We clinked glasses and I wondered what made him think that I loved him. As if he had read my thoughts, after draining his glass and waiting for me to take a sip from mine, he went on, "I know that I've never told you, in so many words, that I love you, Natalia, but, I mean, you must know that I do, and, well, now that we're married, I suppose that, you know, you must love me too, just a little bit at least, don't you?"

I think I blushed then, and to relieve my confusion I took another sip of my wine.

"What I said in the church is what I feel, Natalia. I'm going to love and protect you my whole life long. I'm going to be a good husband, I swear it."

He must have taken my confusion for sheer timidity, because without waiting for me to speak he took the wine glass from my hand, set it on the dinner table, and hugged me tight, pressing his head against my neck. He smelled of manly sweat and tobacco smoke. I remember thinking that I'd have to get used to that smell, because from that moment forth it would be with me for the rest of my life.

"Come," he said, picking me up in his arms and carrying me down the hall as if I weighed no more than a pillow.

The girls had decorated the bed with an ivory-coloured lace bedspread we had brought from Spain, which they had sprinkled with flower petals. Rojo was going to set me down, but I realized that if I lay on the bed then I would crush the flowers and stain the bedspread and my clothes, so I turned in his arms and explained my fear to him, and he let me down on the floor.

We removed the bedspread together. He stood there in his shirtsleeves, looking at me from the other side of the bed as if he didn't know what to do. The sweat stains under his arms nearly reached his waistband. Suddenly he was breathing hard, as if he had been exercising.

"I'm going to the bathroom," I said, because I had to get out of there and be alone for a moment, but he smiled as if that were exactly what he had been waiting to hear.

I went out to the courtyard in the last blue light of day, took a deep breath, and looked at myself in the mirror that we had hung by the door. My hair was somewhat mussed, my cheeks were red, and my eyes shone as if I had a fever, but I found that I looked pretty, and that gave me a bit more confidence.

If it had been Diego waiting for me in the bedroom everything would have been easier. We would have danced for a while, even without any music, and then — and then, I suppose, the same thing would have happened. But it would have been different, very different.

That night I didn't dance. I sent word to Grisela that I wasn't feeling well, and I shut myself up in my flat with two bottles of cane liquor. My plan was to get myself seriously drunk, sitting alone in my only armchair, the one I had bought from a Genoese family when they moved out of the tenement. I held one bottle in my hand and kept my stash of tobacco at my feet like a faithful dog. That was the longest night of my life. The demonic January heat shrouded me in its foetid breath. Voices that rose to my open window made we want to rush out and kill whoever it was who thought there was any reason in the universe for laughter. The world had never seemed so disgusting, so impoverished, so ugly. Closing my eyes, I saw Natalia's figure, dressed in white, like a lily pushing up through the filth of a rubbish dump that was fenced off, closed off to me, unreachable. Drink surged through my blood like fire, devouring without consuming me. I knew that all the water in the world wouldn't suffice to put out this blaze.

Picturing her naked, trembling, crushed under the weight of

that Teutonic giant, who would be rubbing his coarse paws across her silken skin, I shuddered with revulsion, hatred, impotence. Impotence above all. What could I do? What could I, a nobody, do? A nobody to her. If she had at least given me some signal, if she had said she didn't want to get married, said she needed me to free her, I would have confronted the whole world with the dagger I've handled since I was a little boy growing up in the tenements. But she had said nothing, and my love gave me no rights but the right to burn, slowly, alone, thinking about her and what might have been.

Dawn found me in the courtyard under the tree with yellow flowers, wrapped in a sheet that I had taken from the chest of drawers. Tears rolled down my cheeks each time I felt the shooting pain between my legs or that hot, swollen spot that was beating like a heart.

It disgusted me. Even though I had washed myself over and over again with cold water, taking care not to wake up Rojo or Papá, it disgusted me to feel that my body was no longer mine, that my stupid pride in thinking of myself as the perfect little lady had brought me to this, this new breaking day, this house that was not and never would be my house, this country on the other side of the sea.

Now I was a real woman. Now I had everything I had desired: a house, a wedding, a husband. What came next? Watching the years go by, having children, growing old, dying? If I didn't die of sorrow first. Lost in a land that wasn't mine, tied to a man I now knew was not the one I should be with. What was I supposed to think about, now that I was married? What plans could I make when Rojo shipped off to sea and I stayed home with Papá to wait for his return? To wait? Wait for him to come back, after weeks or months had passed, so that he could do to me once more what he had just done?

It had been very nice at first, very sweet. He had cradled me in his arms as delicately as my father might have done. He had caressed my hair and cheeks, repeating my name very softly, *Natalia, Natalia*, again and again, like a prayer. I asked him what he wanted me to call him. He said Rojo or Berstein was O.K., either one, it made no difference to him.

"But you must have a name, haven't you? The one the priest gave you when you were baptised? What your mother called you when you were little?"

"Yes," he said, "but I'm ashamed of it."

"Come on, tell it to me. After all, it's probably German, and I won't be able to pronounce it."

He put his mouth close to my ear and said, "Heini. My Christian name is Heinrich, but they always called me Heini, until I went off to sea."

"What's that in Spanish?"

"Enrique."

"Well, that's not so bad."

"But in German, Heini also means clod, simpleton, you know? Here I'm El Rojo. For you, too."

Then he stopped talking, but he kept on caressing me. He didn't limit himself to touching my hair and face any more. It was as if he had suddenly realized that he was my husband, that I belonged to him. And he seemed in a great hurry to make me understand it.

He turned me around, pressed me against the mattress, and kissed me on the mouth, thrusting a tongue that tasted of beer and cigar smoke between my teeth. I felt like vomiting.

A rosy glow spread across the sky, but it was still dark in the courtyard. I heard a cock crow and I burst into tears. It was my birthday, the day when Grandfather Francesc used to take me by the hand before breakfast and stroll with me, just the two of us, first to Mass and to take communion in the cathedral, then to have churros and hot chocolate across the street from the church of Santa Catalina. I'd wear my best dress and my Sunday coat, and he'd have his frock coat and silk hat, along with his cape and walking stick. Afterwards he'd take me to the old toy store on San Vicente street and let me choose whatever I wanted: a blond doll, a globe, a box of puppets.

On my last birthday before he died, he offered me his arm after we had our breakfast and, on our usual way to the toy store, he suddenly turned a different corner and stopped in front of a jeweller's. He opened the door for me.

"You're nearly a woman now, Natalia," he said. "I think you're too grown up for toys."

And he bought me a ring. The first piece of jewellery I ever owned. The only piece.

Now I had just turned twenty. My present was the pain I felt between my legs. And another ache, much more intense: that of knowing I had made a mistake. And that this error would last for ever.

By the time I realized there was someone else in the courtyard it was too late. Whoever it was, he had to have heard me crying. I shrank into the rocking chair, cocooning myself in the sheet in case it was El Rojo.

But it was my father.

He hugged me clumsily. Then he helped me to my feet, dried my tears with his palm, sat on the rocking chair and took me in his arms, as he used to do when I was very little and he sang songs to help me sleep. And he, the man from Navarre who had never wanted to learn the Valencian language, started whispering into my ear.

Perleta, perleta meva, no ploris, perleta, no ploris.

Don't cry, *perleta meva*. My little pearl. Mamá's pet name for me.

THREE

I met him at a milonga one Saturday in November, just past midnight. The streets lay dark and deserted under a snowfall that had lightly sugared the cars and roofs, creating the ghost-city illusion I knew so well from so many other nights in so many other towns in central Europe, when, leaving the theatre or the concert hall, I would walk to my hotel to change my clothes, grab my dancing shoes and head back outside to look for the dance floor that would once more give meaning to my existence. My nocturnal existence, of which my colleagues knew nothing, thinking me unsociable and excessively conscientious about my responsibilities as first violin.

As I walked along I wondered, with half of my mind, how it was possible that a woman of my age could let herself be carried away like this by her passion for the tango, instead of retiring to her room to wake refreshed and relaxed for the concert in Salzburg the next day. But the other half of my mind simply kept my feet moving along the white-caked sidewalk, wondering, with a glimmer of self-irony, what I expected to find in Landsberg at midnight on a frosty Saturday.

I arrived nearly out of breath, snow sprinkling my shoulders and my nose reddened, and passed through the door of the theatre without stopping to think about it, afraid I'd find the same disappointment I had on other occasions: a poor, sad dance floor, a surplus of women leaning their elbows on the bar, pretending to be indifferent but staring daggers at the woman who had just entered without a partner to compete with them for the few unattached tangueros, men who took turns asking them to dance and made them feel for a few minutes the sweet delirium of surrender to a stranger who picks you up and carries you off and decides for you.

The heat came rushing to my face, and an unexpected wave of nausea washed over me in an instant, leaving me feeling shaky in its wake. There were only two women talking with each other at a small table. On the improvised dance floor staked out in the middle of the Stadttheater foyer for the milonga, seven or eight couples danced with eyes closed in the dimness that was scantly lit by a couple of dozen red candles, the kind people bring to cemeteries to celebrate All Saints' Day.

I took off my overcoat while my eyes adjusted to the darkness. I leaned over to tighten the buckles of my shoes and felt the familiar tickling sensation of someone staring at my movements. I looked up and there he was, on the stairs, like an image ripped from an old print: black trousers, waistcoat crossed by a silver watch chain, white shirt, cravat, hat pulled jauntily low over a pair of intensely burning eyes.

In my tango dreams he must have looked just like this. If I had been a woman of the past century in some hovel in La Boca, this man would have driven me wild. The stories I had told myself on nights spent at different hotels were interwoven with the lyrics of the tangos I knew so well: songs of desertion and estrangement, of tragic, passionate love, of tobacco smoke and rum-drenched nights punctuated by the sweet, sorrowful, rending wail of the bandoneón. But I was a woman of the twenty-first century, and I knew the difference between life and dreams, between stories made up on my lonely nights and the small-bore reality of a snow-covered town. And in this reality, I couldn't be bought so cheap, with an intense stare, a tight waistcoat, a dancer's slender body. Even if he were sincere, perhaps he was only trying to live out his own night-time dream, which would dissipate like night mist at daybreak before the mirror of some drab bedroom suite.

I felt tempted to walk over to him and try a joke about his vintage tanguero costume, but someone had just changed the music. Gardel's muddy voice was singing the opening strains of "Volver", and when I saw him move in bold, fluid steps towards me, my impulse to laugh at him unexpectedly vanished. His eyes were green. They flashed between long, dark lashes. He did not speak, did not smile. He stood before me, tall and straight yet languid, like a leather whip, waiting.

I set aside my unlit cigarette on the table and stepped ahead of him on to the dance floor, sensing in my wake an indefinable aroma, a mixture of old-fashioned cologne and black tobacco. A warm sensation hit the back of my neck and spread down my icy spine.

I'd danced before with shady characters, old-school machos, the sort of professional *porteños* who exaggerate their Argentine accents to make you understand that you've found the real article, what you've been looking for your whole nocturnal life as a single woman who loves the tango. When I turned around to let him embrace me, I was ready to hear his hoarse, languid voice asking me what was my name, where had I appeared from, what was a nice woman like me doing in a place like this.

He didn't say a word. He put his hand on my back and the music wrapped around us like a silk handkerchief. For a moment I felt his breath against my cheek, and suddenly the hall and the couples around us and even the very floor we danced on ceased to exist. Never before had I felt such passion for the dance. All my experience, all my years of dancing tango, all the courses I had taken in Buenos Aires dissolved in his presence. I was simply a soul, dancing, dangling from a sorcerer's spell, flying and sinking, following his light like a nocturnal butterfly. In his arms my body grew supple and submissive, yielding to his desires before my mind consciously picked up on them. It was like being in another world, like being both alive and dead, and at the same time yearning that it would never end, that this state of grace might never be broken.

I don't know if I closed my eyes. I remember the texture of his waistcoat, the play of his shoulder muscles, the warmth of his hand against my back. I don't know if we danced for hours or minutes or centuries. I know that at some point he took off his hat and I saw his black hair glistening with brilliantine, his tanned young face with deep, vertical wrinkles like razor cuts down his cheeks, and his half-closed eyes watching me with such passion as I shall never encounter again.

We danced. Danced the music, danced the stories I had told myself, danced memories of a time gone by that I had never known. We danced nostalgia and grief and madness and the only words between us were the words of the songs we danced. What could we have said to one another? When two people speak without words, what needs to be said aloud? Should I have told him about my nomadic life, about the hotels and the contracts and the envy of my colleagues? Was he going to tell me about his nostalgia, about his underpaid work in some dance studio, about the European women who saw in him the fiery and temperamental Latin lover they had been searching for, someone who would take them briefly out of their comfortable routines until they grew frightened of what they were doing and dropped him?

A cheery, playful milonga had just started playing when a rose peddler came up to us, an African teenager with a dazzling smile. He waved over the peddler without thinking, then grimaced and returned his hand to my back. But the boy pulled out a rose and offered it to us, happy to be selling one flower after so many tries, so many polite refusals, so many eyes avoiding his. He shook his head as if it pained him to disappoint the African vendor, but then, a second before the boy caught on, he quickly took off his watch and handed it over in exchange for the flower. The boy smiled again and gave him the flower without accepting the trade, then slapped him on the shoulder, uttered a few words I couldn't hear, and wandered away amongst the tables.

He then snapped off the stem and placed the flower in my hair, viewing me with pride, as if I were his and he were decking me out for a ceremony. I pulled my handkerchief from the cut in my dress, not knowing why, and held it to his lips. He kissed it with a smile, his first smile of the night, and folded it in his breast pocket like a magician's prop, fanning its lace edge against the black cloth of his coat.

Perhaps it lasted only a few seconds, but this scene is so deeply engraved in my memory that when I close my eyes I can see it like a film, all in black and white except for the red rose. Then a milonga drew us back in, and then another tango, and then some songs by Pugliese — "Yuyo verde", "Farol", "Recuerdo", especially "Recuerdo" — that made him close his eyes and grit his teeth, as if he were recalling something painful and distant.

At some point I reluctantly noticed a general movement in the hall. I held on to him as if he would otherwise dissolve into air. Time was up. Couples started separating and saying their goodbyes to acquaintances. Others blew out the candles and gathered up the C.D.s they had been playing all night long. The tinkling of the last drinks could be heard over the music, the conversations of couples making plans for Sunday afternoon, breakfast invitations. Minutes slipped away like pearls from a broken necklace. I didn't want it to end. After being in that other world, I'd have to return to reality now, a reality that I could tell would be nasty: a snowstorm that must have grown more intense, the cold outdoors, the words that would come, that would necessarily have to come, whether to say goodbye or to leave together for my hotel, to exchange addresses or to decide if we were going to his place or mine, where do you live, do you have a car, what do you want to do. When all I really wanted was to stay on here, to keep dancing, for the night never to end, not to become a casual lover, but for him always to be the stranger who helped me discover the passion for the tango that I had thought I already knew.

The music stopped. We pulled apart slowly, painfully, as if the time we had spent together had been enough to turn us into a single being. I looked down at my shoes, then glanced off at the window that separated us from the world outdoors. With a half-smile, he nodded his head as if pointing me towards the chair where I had left my boots, while he turned to the table where his hat was waiting.

I watched him put it on slowly, adjusting the angle over his left eye, and take another look at me, from far away, a long glance full of words that I didn't know how to hear. Then he disappeared into the shadows at the other end of the hall. I tied my boots as slowly as possible, expecting to see him walk back my way before I finished. But I had time to lace my boots, put on my overcoat, pick up the handbag I had been carrying the whole time we were dancing, and light a cigarette.

An older man, probably the milonga organizer, came over to tell me that they had to shut down, that it was almost four in the morning, and that he hoped I had not found the music or the atmosphere disappointing. I thanked him, not daring to ask whether there was another exit in the rear of the hall, whether someone should check to see if there might be anyone left behind in the men's room before they locked up.

A minute later I was in the street, standing in snow that had been pockmarked by the tracks of all the couples who had just left the dance, shifting my weight from one foot to the other, calling myself an idiot for not speaking up, for not knowing whether I should keep waiting there, like a dog without an owner, for someone who had promised me nothing. I lit another cigarette and smoked it down to the filter, feeling the cold grow more and more intense despite my overcoat, twirling the rosebud that I had just plucked from my hair where he had placed it. I didn't even know his name or his address or the slightest bit of information that might lead me to him if I lost track of him now.

I waited for nearly half an hour, knowing he would never come, that it was impossible to pretend this was just a misunderstanding. I looked through the posters over the door in an effort to penetrate the darkness on the other side of the glass and perhaps discern a light at the back of the hall. One of the posters announced the next milonga, a few days before Christmas, on a Saturday that I would be spending in London.

I walked slowly back to the hotel, floating in the memory of the most beautiful thing that had ever happened to me and at the same time wallowing in self-pity for my loss, for the humiliation of being abandoned. The night porter handed me a note: the bus would be picking us up at a quarter past seven, after breakfast.

Back in my room, I looked at myself in the mirror, thinking that if the night had turned out differently there would now be a double image here, his white body contrasting with his tanned face, my blond tresses next to his polished black hair. Refusing to let myself think about it any longer, I emptied my handbag of money, lipstick, cigarettes, hotel card. I took off my dress and was about to pack it in my suitcase when I realized that something had fallen to the floor. It was a visiting card, antique typography on yellowed paper: "Diego Monteleone", it said. Underneath, an address in Buenos Aires, crossed out, and in a small, masculine hand (as my primary-school teacher used to say) was written, in pencil, another address in the district of La Boca.

* * *

It took me more than three months to extricate myself from my contracts and fly to Argentina. It didn't surprise anyone that I would need a few days off, but in any event it had been weeks since I cared what might or might not surprise my colleagues. Diego had made a date with me and that was all that mattered.

No sooner had I moved into the hotel than I grabbed a taxi and gave the driver the address. It took us more than an hour to get from the Florida district to La Boca, crossing street after street, each one shabbier and emptier than the last, until we reached a street that only a tourist could find picturesque.

The street number on the calling card belonged to a small house with windows that had not been cleaned in a long time and decaying wooden walls that might once have been blue. The cabby turned to me with worry in his face.

"Did you really mean to stop here, madam?"

I asked him to wait for me and got out of the taxi. A strong wind, reeking of rot and stagnant seawater, swept bits of paper, dry leaves and litter along the street and around my legs. I rapped several times with my knuckles, but the house was empty, seemingly deserted.

"Are there any tango studios in this area?" I asked the man. "Any milongas you've heard of?"

"Around the corner there, on Caminito, there's a couple of good spots, but it's too early still. You'll have to wait an hour or two."

I asked him for his phone number so I could call him when I was ready to leave the district, and let him go.

"If you don't have anything to do to pass the time," he told me before driving off, "on the next street over, the one that passes by the wharves, you've got the Quinquela Martín Museum. All the tourists come here to see it."

When he drove off in the cloud of dust raised by the wind, I felt as if I had been abandoned in the desert. But I knew that Diego had to be here, very close by. Somewhere near here he was shining his dance shoes, combing brilliantine into his jet-black hair, waiting for the moment, waiting for nightfall so he could enter the milonga and find me there.

Both tango spots were closed, their chairs turned upside-down on the tables, their bars clear and gleaming like highways to nowhere.

The museum was open but empty, almost desolate, abandoned like a cemetery where no-one brings flowers any more. I bought an entrance ticket from a listless little deaf man who sat there reading a sports paper and ventured into the lonely galleries, my footsteps echoing through the labyrinth, my gaze wandering across paintings that had been hung without any discernible plan on walls painted in sad pink, sickly yellow, deathly green.

I had no desire to look at Quinquela's works. All I wanted was to leave that place and find Diego, or else go back to my hotel, to the city centre, to the hustle and bustle of the capital with its shops and bars.

I paused between two possible paths to the exit from that dusty, decrepit place. And then I saw him.

On a bilious wall, between two horrendously sad, dull paintings, his green eyes fixed me in a fiery stare from under the black brim of his hat.

I moved closer, almost on tiptoe, as if afraid to wake a sleeping child. Because it was him. I knew it was him. The man who had given me the rose that I still carried with me everywhere, who had embraced my body at the milonga, who had made me fly above the music. But I had to make certain, because things like this don't really happen, because only in dreams and in the stories I used to tell myself at night were there men who dressed in black suits with silver pocket watches, who had strong arms and slender bodies, who smelled of old-fashioned cologne and black tobacco. Because only in my nightmares was there always a man who danced the tango like a god and who wore in his waistcoat pocket, lightly grazing it with his fingertip, as if to be sure it was still there, the lace handkerchief with my initial embroidered in red. And who looked at me proudly, knowing me, recognizing me, because I had come in search of him.

Under the painting, on a small plate, rusted around the edges, I could decipher: "*Tango is a lasting wound*. Unknown artist. Ca. 1920."

FOUR

Saying goodbye to Natalia right after our wedding was the hardest thing I've done in my life. And it's not as if my life has been an easy one. Tell the truth, it only started getting on track after one of those chance events that sometimes happen to you — when I got on a ship bound for Argentina, discovered that I liked the sea, and became a sailor.

It wasn't the first time she'd waved goodbye to me from the wharf. Sometimes she'd come with other girls, sometimes with her father, but those other times Natalia had only been my girlfriend, my fiancée, a pretty little teenage girl I could aspire to but had no rights over. After so many failures in my life, I still couldn't believe it might be different now. When I watched Natalia from on board the *Southern Star* it was like watching a dream, knowing that sooner or later you'd have to wake up and realize it had all been a lie, you were still alone, with men and cables and cargo, nobody to love, nobody who cared about you.

But on that day, watching her from the ship, her in her dress as blue as a piece of summer sky, I finally began to believe that luck was smiling on me. The woman waving her hand at me from there on the wharf was my wife, the one who'd always be waiting in La Boca for me to return, the one who'd give me children, the one who'd keep me company in my old age when the sea was nothing more than a memory.

My breath quickened when I recalled the night before: her white, smooth body, offered up to me on the bed, her modesty, her innocence, her mane of fragrant hair spreading over the pillow, dark and serene, like the forests of my homeland.

For many months I'd have to be without her. Worse still, without any news of her. But it was still better than all the times that had come before, because now Natalia was mine for ever, and she was a good girl who'd wait for me in Buenos Aires until I got back.

I worried about my father-in-law's illness, above all because he had told me very clearly, in our conversation before the wedding, that he didn't have much time left and that Natalia did not know it, he had never wished to lay that burden on her. He also explained to me that he had no savings. What he was spending on our wedding was practically all he had. He even offered to let me withdraw my marriage proposal, because Natalia had no dowry and nothing saved for a rainy day. But we sailors in La Boca were like a big family, and I was convinced that, if the worst came to pass, Natalia would be safe until I got back because she could live decently on my salary. I had scarcely any expenses and was ready to do without the little luxuries I had allowed myself as a bachelor so that she would have everything she might need.

But it broke my heart to watch her from the *Star*, growing smaller and smaller as we sailed into the distance, with her father ill, before I'd had enough time to make her truly mine, other than that one time on our wedding night.

Whenever I let down my guard, the tango lyrics that were coming into fashion then would fill my head, shameless songs about betrayals and insults and decent women who grew tired of being poor and wasting their lives in tenements and slums, who threw themselves at the first man with cash who would take them for a ride in his motor car. Marco used to sing those tangos at night, strumming along on his guitar. I had to give him a couple of punches once to get him to shut up.

I couldn't keep myself from recalling the guy who'd danced with Natalia at the wedding. My blood boiled. I'd done it with the best intentions. I hadn't wanted to make a spectacle in front of my father-in-law and all the guests by forbidding the woman who had just become my wife from showing herself off with another man.

When all is said and done, dancing is normal at a wedding. I didn't want to deny Natalia the pleasure of enjoying, decently, a couple of tangos in front of her father and all the neighbours. But that stuck-up little *compadrito* with his polished hair — he had such a gleam in his eyes that it turned my stomach and made me think about daggers flickering in the light of a street lamp.

Off at sea, under the moon, surrounded by men, the thought of those songs was like a dagger in my back, an intense pain that kept me up late and then brought nightmares in which Natalia, in a short, tight skirt and holding a cigarette, danced the tango in a cabaret under the dirty stares of men in tailcoats and bow ties. Those days I'd wake up full of bile, ready to bash in the snout of anybody who got in my way. And sometimes I did. My men would quietly wipe the blood from their noses, spit overboard, and avoid my eyes. Then I'd be disgusted with myself and hole myself up in my cabin for a few hours, until my anger went down and I convinced myself it was nothing but a dream brought on by jealousy and the anguish of being so far from her. I'd think of the moment I met her, at sixteen, sailing with her father for the first time. As I concentrated on the sparkle in her dark eyes and the grace of her figure, the beast within me would slowly calm down. Until all of a sudden any little thing re-awakened it, a red veil fell over me, and once more the beast roared.

I would have given anything to know how to write so I could send her love letters from every port of call, but I'd never gone to school and the only fellow on the *Star* who knew how to read was the captain, and he only enough to decipher cargo lists and contracts.

Anyway, I didn't want to put myself in his hands. I didn't want anyone to find out about my love for Natalia and mock me for it, because if life had taught me anything it was that a man who lets anybody get away with taunting him, who isn't ready to make him pay for a snub, loses his authority.

My father had been a tinsmith. My whole childhood, we'd wandered, town to town, city to city, fixing pots, making just enough to survive. Sometimes, not even that. My mother died giving birth to me, in Landsberg. We'd go back to that town sometimes, because the people there were friendly and they already knew us. The few good memories I have from my early years are from there, from that little city with its colourful houses, its ancient towers, its beautiful river slipping quietly, like a tame animal, past green, tree-lined banks.

We spent many years in Innsbruck and Landsberg, the only two cities that made any impact on me. I get all the others mixed up, between the muddy roads, the packed snow that I'd slip on, or the icy mud that would seep into my patched and repatched shoes.

I never had time to learn how to read, or how to do anything but survive, use my fists, and handle a blade.

When my father died, I joined up with some Italian comedy actors and headed with them to Genoa. From there I sailed to Argentina, starting off as a cabin boy and working my way up to boatswain, seeing one port after another, much as I had once seen towns and hamlets on foot, until they all started to look like painted scenes to me, stage props made of rags and cardboard, always with the same drunks, stevedores, whores and sailors. Until I met Natalia and decided, for her sake, to make a gentleman of myself.

It was a long, wet summer. Once the excitement and bustle of the wedding were past, its preparations and mysteries, we went back to life as usual. I now slept in the big bed, in what used to be Papá's room, but otherwise nothing had changed at home. We continued to eat dinner together, though at times the cutlery now seemed a little heavier, and we might look at each other in an uncomfortable silence we had never known before, as if he suddenly didn't know how to talk to me. At such moments I thought it would almost have been better if Rojo hadn't been a sailor, if he sat down to eat lunch and supper every day with us, until all of us, even me, accepted the fact that we, who had always been two, were now three. But at other times — most of the time — I was happy that Berstein wasn't there, and I fervently hoped that his journey would last weeks and months, until all that remained of him was a blurry memory and the ring I wore on my finger.

The neighbours also treated me differently. The change was subtle, but I felt it, and it amazed me that the one unpleasant night

I had spent with Rojo weeks ago should have worked this change, this glimmer of respect that I had never commanded before, these approving gazes, as if I were a fruit tree or a milk cow that was developing nicely and held some promise for the future.

The Italian girls tried to wheedle me into telling them about my glorious wedding night, but I gave nothing away and only went along with them to the extent of dealing out half-smiles and comments on the importance of keeping it a surprise.

I had heard nothing more about Diego, though I asked about him very discreetly. It seemed that no-one had seen him around. All I was able to find out was that he was a newsman, that he danced every night in theatres and cafés, and that he was having a lot of problems with his dancing partner and was thinking about looking for a replacement. I heard this in Uxío's shop, from the same musicians who had serenaded me the night before the wedding. While I waited for the shopkeeper to refill the bottle with red wine, with my back turned to the table where they were playing cards, I strained to understand what they were saying whenever I heard Diego's name mentioned.

Everything about my life had stayed the same, but still something had changed, something that made me restless and forced me out into the courtyard many nights after Papá had retired to bed. Our home, which had always been my refuge, was now collapsing on top of me, overwhelming me.

On nights like that, pacing back and forth across the flower-filled courtyard, I would dream of transforming into a falcon and flying over the sleeping city, drunk with freedom, listening to the tango music that flowed from the cafés, the dance halls, the confectionery shops, the theatres . . . All Buenos Aires had become a tango, while I had to embrace myself, alone, in the shadows of the courtyard.

Ever since I had danced with that man on my wedding day I had found no rest. His memory was like a creeping vine that had set roots in my heart and was coiling around me from the inside, growing stronger and stronger, slowly bringing down the wall that supported my life, until every stone was broken.

Sometimes I thought that perhaps my problem was that I wasn't the decent woman I had always believed. But I felt that the house was growing too small for me, that I had been struck with a harpoon in the centre of my chest and someone was hauling in the line, dragging me to places that I could hardly imagine and that would be my perdition.

And El Rojo, who might have stopped it, wasn't coming back. Rojo wasn't coming back. Papá had started coughing and spitting blood once more. And I had never seen Diego again.

"A crush," Doña Melina had said, "a passing infatuation." Passing? Something that had already gone on for three months? Something that was consuming me like a sickness, like a fire, roasting me slowly from within so that no-one could see it, leaving me weak and ashamed?

"It's because she misses her husband," said the Italian girls whenever anyone at the marketplace remarked that I looked pale and haggard. Or they'd joke about a possible pregnancy. But I knew that neither guess was true. I just lowered my head and let the older women think whatever they wished.

Summer seemed as if it would never end. Each night I danced like mad, holding tight to Grisela's body, which weighed less and less, became fragile, transparent, like the body of a sparrow. I immersed myself in the tango with all the mad desperation of the bitterness that gnawed at me from within. Closing my eyes, I dreamt it was Natalia dancing with me. Better than opening them wide to see the reality that surrounded me in that café on Maipú street: Grisela's blurred gaze, the bruises over her body, the false cheer of gangs of rich kids from the best families spending more in a night than she or I could make in a lifetime, cocaine-filled salt cellars on marble café tables, waiters dressed as women . . . Buenos Aires, the great cosmopolitan metropolis, the most European city in the Americas, had become an image of hell, and I travelled through it, my hat at a jaunty angle and a dagger in my hand, knowing that paradise was on Necochea street but not for me. That's why I went by La Boca as little as possible, and always late, very late at night, so I'd never run into Natalia by accident.

I had heard from Yuyo that her father was sick in the lungs, so they'd had to take him to the Spanish Hospital, the one with the nuns, and she'd been left alone, barely earning enough to live on from the sewing piecework that Yuyo brought her. Her husband's salary all went to pay for the medicine. Not that it did any good, except maybe to put off the old man's death a while so he could suffer longer and she could slip further into poverty.

One autumn afternoon I lost Grisela. They told me at the newspaper office. By the time I got to her tenement room, they'd already cut the poor girl down from the beam where she'd hanged herself. There weren't even half a dozen of us at her funeral. I bought some flowers at a street stall and left them there in her grave, because I thought she would have liked it. I felt ashamed that it had never occurred to me to buy her flowers while she was alive.

After I lost my dance partner I started making the rounds of the local cafés and cabarets, just another tanguero. My dreams of glory, of dancing in the theatres of Europe some day, were fading. My memories of a world where something like happiness might exist slipped further and further away.

But so long as Buenos Aires was full of noise and trams, and they talked about building a second underground tube line, like in Paris, and women cut their hair short and their skirts shorter, I went on wallowing in the cafés, from brothels to billiard halls, back to my origins as a *compadrito*, already old before my time at the age of twenty-five.

"My father is dead. Papá is dead." In my head I repeated these words over and over, like a prayer, trying to convince myself that it was true, as if it weren't enough that the coffin sat in the middle of the drawing room surrounded by four fat yellow candles, as if it weren't enough that I could see him in it, his face growing thinner by the hour, his skin turning colder, paler, more transparent, telling me at every moment that he was drifting further away and leaving me alone, forsaken, with an absent husband whom I scarcely knew, with an empty home.

From the hall I could hear the hum of conversations among the neighbours who smoked in front of the door. The women neighbours sitting around me on low stools they had brought from their houses, were reciting whispered prayers. From time to time someone would approach me with murmured words of condolence that I could barely understand.

The damp air, hot from the candles that had been lit throughout the room, was making me dizzy. Everything smelled of sadness, of poverty, of having reached the end of a dark, narrow tunnel from which I would never emerge.

I wished I could have run into the streets screaming, tearing off my clothes, until I jumped naked into the river, wished the ocean that had brought me to this strange city would take me in and cleanse me of all my grief and humiliation and finally return me to the distant land I should never have left. But no, I could do nothing but stay there, where I was, feeling the tears drip down my cheeks, making an effort to keep anyone from hearing me weep.

At some time during that endless night Doña Melina came up to me. She was now but a poor, faded woman, beaten down by the sorrow of losing her only daughter, my poor María Esther, who had died in childbirth along with her baby. She hugged me so tight that the rosary around her neck bored an impression into my chest. I remember feeling ashamed, even through my fog of grief and helplessness, that María Esther had died while I remained alive. Doña Melina parted from me, with a light touch on my cheek. A moment later she vanished, a ghost. We had no time to speak.

By three in the morning almost all the neighbours had left, promising to come back after sunrise to pick up the coffin and carry it to the church. Two old women, strangers to me, had nodded off in their rush chairs. The candles had burned down until their flames had gone out, drowning in their own wax, dying with a sputter, as in the cathedral of Valencia at the end of a novena, when the sacristan went around dousing the last candles, kicking out the last church ladies, locking all the doors.

I stood up, feeling light, unlike myself, as if I were the one who had died, and walked around the dark hall, searching for a bit of fresh air by the door that was still ajar. Rain fell meekly, rhythmically, monotonously, as if it had all the time in the universe to finish flooding the earth.

At that moment, watching it rain, I thought — and it seemed I wasn't the one doing the thinking — that there was now no-one left who cared that I was alive, and for an instant, in addition to my sorrow and loneliness, I felt something for which I had no name: something like relief, because no-one had a right any longer to expect anything from me. I didn't think about Rojo.

Then I heard the sound of a throat clearing in the street, and Yuyo showed up, the skinny squeezebox player who had become a sort of friend, the one who had brought me the piecework that I had hoped would earn me enough to save Papá — the boy from that serenade, which seemed to have happened in some other life, to some other girl. Behind him, unexpectedly, like an apparition, I saw the face of another man, pale, serious. My stomach leapt.

Both men removed their hats. Yuyo repeated the same words I had been hearing for so many hours: "My condolences, madam. Don Joaquín was a good man. At least his suffering is over."

The other man, who was not Diego, said nothing. He lowered his head and followed Yuyo into the drawing room.

I had to sit down, right there in the hall, because my legs would not support me.

When the squeezebox player told me Natalia's father had died, for an instant I thought I might go down and pay my respects. I'd never have a better occasion to see her. The thought even passed through my head that I could ask her to be my dance partner, because I knew that she'd need the money and that her husband was off at sea. But it would have been an insult. She was a married lady, not one of the desperate girls I hung around with. A real lady couldn't dance in public with a man who wasn't her husband, even if she wanted to.

So I got together with Malena, a lively brunette who drew stares from every man in the room. Thanks to her, half a dozen elegant cafés hired us. But it was only my body dancing. My soul, or the bit of soul still left to me after I lost Natalia, would take to the air whenever the tango started, flying me far, far away, to a dark, fragrant, velvety place, where she was waiting for me, holding out her hand for me, her eyes half closed and a hint of a smile on her lips.

That's how I always imagined her, I don't know why: wearing black dancing clothes, hair done up in a chignon with a tortoise-shell comb, leaning against the jamb of a door that opened one way on to the milonga and the other on to a night-time garden, waiting for me. The image was so clear, so intense, it seemed like a child-hood memory. An impossible memory from a past that had never taken place. That's why, sometimes, when I was trying to motivate myself, I'd pretend it was maybe a memory of the future, of what life had in store for me, even if things were going against me for now.

One night at Salón Peracca, during the break, a guy came up to me. I'd seen him all evening, leaning against a column with a notebook in his hands, and I'd noticed him a few nights earlier at La Puñalada. At first I thought he might be a fellow newspaperman, but soon I realized, from the way he was watching us dance, that he had to be in some other line of work.

"Señor Monteleone?" he asked.

"The same."

"I have a proposal to make you. May I buy you a drink?"

We went to the bar, sizing each other up. Me, my stomach in a knot, thinking he must be some sort of agent who wanted to hire us; he, smiling and at peace, leading me to guess that his proposal wouldn't signify much of a change in my life.

"My name is Nicanor Urías. I am a painter."

We ordered two glasses of gin. The guy must have noticed my

puzzlement, because he quickly added, "I would like to paint a series of portraits on the subject of the tango, and you caught my eye. I would like you to model for me. I will pay you well, if you are willing to pose a few times in my *atelier*. As for the hours, whatever is most convenient for you."

"How much?"

"A hundred pesos for five sessions. If it takes more sessions, thirty pesos each."

The guy had to be off his rocker. My flat cost me forty-five a month. If this wasn't a con, I'd just solved three months of rent.

"Why me?"

"Because I like you." He saw me recoil and hurriedly said, "Don't get me wrong, *compadre*, I'm not one of those. What I like is your shape, that chiselled face, your stare, your expression, do you know what I mean? I've never seen anyone who embodies the spirit of the tango as you do."

"Don't you also need a woman?" I asked, thinking of Natalia and how handy it would be for her to make that kind of dough, never needing to know that it had come to her through me.

"I already have one in mind, but thanks." From the way he glanced at Malena, I guessed that he thought I was talking about her and that, for whatever reason, she wasn't right for him. Though when I saw her at that moment, following the painter's eyes, I also realized that, although Malena was what we called a lioness in my district — a real woman, as the Gallegos would say — she wasn't the spirit of the tango, in his words. The spirit of the tango was Natalia, and suddenly I didn't want him to know it.

"Well?"

"Agreed."

We shook hands, finished our drinks, and he gave me his address. Then the break ended and I found myself once more on the dance floor, my body turned to tango, my soul far, far away.

When I came home from church after the funeral and shut myself up alone in the house, I felt something I had never felt before: utter helplessness, such loneliness as I wouldn't have believed I could possibly hold inside without dying too. I'm not sure how long I cried, but it must have been a long time because next thing I knew I realized I was hungry and couldn't remember when I had eaten last.

So, what with my grief and my self-pity and my shame at feeling hungry with Papá barely two days dead, I decided that I had to keep going, had to serve myself some of the vegetable stew that I still had stored away and get back to doing the piecework that Yuyo had brought me and keep breathing and washing my face and going to sleep at night in the bed that wasn't mine, in that house that was too big for me by myself, where everything reminded me of Papá and the two short years we had lived there.

Then all the days merged into one: getting up, buying a little bread and milk, sewing, sewing, sewing. Sometimes by myself, sometimes with the Italian girls, who would laugh and gossip around me until they remembered that I was in mourning and fell silent again.

I had no news from El Rojo and one fine day I realized that I'd never even asked whether he knew how to read and write.

Once a week I would go to the shipping company to collect his wages, lining up with all the sailors' wives, then go by the market and return home. I rarely went to church because it was full of sad, lonely women, all in mourning like me. The few saints in the church were also sad and poor and looked as lonely as we did.

Winter came, expenses went up, coal was dear, and I had to make do with a small charcoal brazier to warm my legs while I sewed. I had heard nothing about Diego. I would have fallen apart with embarrassment if I had tried to ask Yuyo about him, and after Papá died I no longer had an excuse for going to Uxío's shop. He was still stuck inside me, like an infected thorn. I was often overcome by dizziness, walking home from the market, when I would turn a corner and see a man who reminded me of him, the way he moved, the play of sunlight on his hair.

I was going soft and sad, like a fig in the fruit basket that no-one feels like eating. I noticed it and felt sorry for myself, but I didn't know what I could do to change.

So that morning, when I went to collect the wages, it took me a long time to react when Don Julián, the shipping company book-keeper, asked me into his office, because I had gone slow and lost the habit of speaking and listening to what I heard around me.

"What?" was as much as I could say. I groped blindly for a chair to sit down.

The man rounded his enormous dark wooden desk, pulled out a straight-backed chair for me, adjusted the pince-nez on his crooked nose, and mumbled something like "I'm sorry, madam," which for some reason sounded completely out of place to me.

"Excuse me," I said when I felt able to speak again, "I don't think I've properly understood you."

The bookkeeper returned to his spot behind the desk, straightened his white oversleeves, and played for a few moments with the black rubber eyeshade he had set on the desk when he saw me enter his office.

"We don't know for certain what happened. We were expecting the *Southern Star* to reach Salvador da Bahia on the fifteenth, but it never arrived. We have learned that it set sail from Tenerife on the anticipated date, but after that — nothing. It disappeared. We didn't say anything to the families until now, because there was still a possibility that a storm had thrown it off course or pushed it towards the coast of Africa, but by now . . ."

It was so hot in that office. I noticed I was suffocating in my tight-collared black dress, with the long mourning veil pushed back over my shoulders. I would have given anything for a glass of water, but it didn't occur to me to ask for one. I looked at the clasped hands in my lap as if they didn't belong to me, and tried to understand what exactly it was that this man was trying to tell me. That Rojo had died, too, like my father? That I was a widow? That I was alone, once and for all?

"Believe me, I am sorry," Don Julián insisted. "You hadn't been married long, had you?"

"In January it would have been one year," I said, my mouth dry, surprised that so much time had already passed.

The bookkeeper closed his eyes for an instant, as if concentrating to form a question that he didn't want to ask. I turned to peer out of the window, which looked out on to a small back courtyard, dark and dirty, filled with unrecognizable rubbish.

". . . family?" I heard, as if from a great distance. "Did you? Have any — any family?"

The word was one I recognized, but it sounded as odd to me as if he had said "parallelepiped" or "solfatara" or any of those words one learns in school and then forgets their meaning.

"My father died in June."

"Oh dear. Dear me. My deepest sympathies, madam. However, what I — I meant to ask, whether you and your husband had children."

"It has barely been seven months since my wedding, Don Julián."

"Yes, of course, excuse me. But you're not . . . ?"

I looked at him uncomprehendingly. He stared back at me. The situation grew more and more embarrassing.

"With child?" Don Julián finally completed his question with a visible effort.

"With child?" I repeated, looking down at my flat stomach, swathed in the black dress of deep mourning, two tightly clasped hands lying across it like a dead butterfly.

"With child, madam. Pregnant. Expecting." The man was starting to lose patience.

I blushed. I felt my ears turning red, felt the heat rising in my cheeks and chest, and was furious that he would notice.

"No, Don Julián. I mean, I don't think so. It's been seven months since I saw — saw my husband," I managed to say, trying to maintain my dignity. "Why do you ask?"

The bookkeeper pulled up his oversleeves again, shifted papers about, picked up a purple pencil and a moment later stuck it behind his left ear with a fluid and unconscious motion. He had an ink stain on his index finger and thumb.

"You see, Señora Berstein." It was the first time I had heard anyone call me by Rojo's name, and I almost burst out laughing. "The company has a compensation and pension fund for the families of its sailors, in case of demise or permanent disability, but as you had been married for so short a time and had no offspring . . . I am sorry, truly sorry."

It took me several seconds to realize the meaning of his words.

"So," I began, and had to clear my throat loudly, because it was so dry, because I didn't know how to go on. Papá had always taken care of these matters. "My husband's wages . . ."

"The company will pay the wages he was due, through the last month worked, no worries. You may come back on Saturday."

"And after that?" The voice that emerged from me was so weak, so timid, I was ashamed of myself, but I felt unable to control it.

Don Julián turned his hands palms up and slightly shrugged. I stared at the papers scattered across the desk as if the solution to my future life lay in them, while silence stretched out between us. I knew there was nothing else to say, but I couldn't stand up and leave the office. My knees had turned to rubber, and my whole body shook.

"I know this is a hard blow," the man said at last, "but you are very young, dear. You will put your life together again, believe me."

How? I wanted to scream at that man. How am I going to put together a life that I never had to start with? How am I going to keep from dying of hunger and loneliness in a strange land, with no family, no friends, no-one who cares what happens to me?

"If you would prefer," said the bookkeeper, standing up, "we could also exchange Señor Berstein's final wages for a return ticket to Spain on one of our freighters. A ship is leaving for Cádiz in two weeks. Think it over, Señora Berstein."

"I'm not Señora Berstein any more," I said in a low voice, holding on to the desk to stand.

"Of course you are."

"Aren't I his widow?"

Don Julián just looked at me across his desk.

"There is no evidence to verify his death."

"What . . . what does that mean?"

"That until the bodies of the crew have been recovered, or until the legal waiting period is past, you are still a married woman."

"The legal waiting period?"

"The law stipulates ten years. If I can do anything else to help you . . ."

He rounded his desk once more, took me by the elbow and, slowly but firmly, led me towards the exit.

"Time goes by quickly, as you'll see" — one step — "and, given that you are in mourning for your father already" — two more steps — "and now, with the loss of your husband" — we were almost at the door — "I doubt you will feel up to remarrying" — his hand on the knob, the door opening onto a grey hallway with a wooden bench on which other women were waiting, wide-eyed, surrounded by small children — "but later on, you'll see. Or, think about the company's offer, and return home. There you'll have family, people who love you; we'll keep you informed if anything turns up. Good morning, Señora Berstein."

Another woman, her eyes wide open, with a baby in her arms and a little girl clutching her skirt, stood up and entered the office that I had just left.

I knew almost all the women waiting on the bench by sight, but

I didn't want to sit with them and talk about my misfortune, so I pulled up the thick black veil that I had thrown over my shoulders when I entered the office, covered my face, and left the building with a drunken gait while the women whispered behind my back.

I was almost at the door to my house when I realized two things all of a sudden: that I had no memory of how I had got there, and that I hadn't shed a tear.

The storm caught up with us along the coast of Brazil after a voyage where everything had gone wrong. The *Star* sank in a matter of minutes, almost before we had time to understand we were really lost. All I remember are huge roaring waves that surged over us in the darkness, the shouts of the men who already figured they were as good as dead, and the creaking and cracking of timbers and derricks, snapping like toothpicks crunched in a giant's jaws. I don't even know what happened to us, if it was just the sea roiled up by a passing cyclone, or an unseen reef that scraped a hole in our hull, or a blow from the tail of some sea monster, as Marco screamed before he disappeared, swallowed up by darkness.

At moments like that you don't think. Anything could be true.

The only thing I do know is that I grabbed on to a broken mast and held tight, along with a fellow sailor, Ochoa the engineer, who complained all night long while the waves churned and shook us and hardly gave us time to breathe, and around us the few other survivors floated away until they were lost to sight.

At some point it was just me left. I closed my eyes, and when I opened them again Ochoa wasn't there any more. The body of the sea was like an enormous animal breathing under me, making me rise and fall at its whim, and overhead the grey sky starting to glow pink.

I believe I saw four mornings dawn before the current swept me close enough to some coast that, in spite of my thirst, cold, hunger and exhaustion, I managed to swim to shore.

I've never been afraid of death, and during those days I discovered that at any other moment in my life I would have let go of the broken mast that held me up and carried me along on the waves. If I didn't, it wasn't out of fear, it was just because the image of Natalia was etched on my memory and had taken the place of all the church images of the Virgin that when I was little had stood in for my mother's face, which I never got to see.

Natalia's image kept me company through those cold, dark hours, like a tiny light at an altar, and gave me the strength to resist, to get back to her, not to leave her all alone now that she had found someone who would protect her and support her, because if there was anyone in the world who knew what it meant to be alone it was me, and I didn't ever want the oath I had sworn to be in vain.

"But would it really hurt you so much to try?" Dolores had asked me. She was another girl from Spain, a little older than me, whom I met one Sunday when Beatrice persuaded me to go with her to a creamery.

Beatrice's fiancé was still off at sea. Lonely, unable to go out dancing or strolling with the single girls, she got so bored, and she insisted so much that I should go out with her for coffee and ensaimadas, that I finally agreed, though I could hardly spare the twenty centavos it would cost me. But she was still living with her parents and brother and earning a bit of cash from her sewing, so she told me it would be on her. We went to La Martona, on Avenida de Mayo in the city centre, a place I hadn't set foot in since poor María Esther's wedding.

There we met Dolores, from Huelva. She had a touch of the woman of the streets about her, which I didn't like at first, but after we started talking and telling our stories, it eventually dawned on me that not every girl would resign herself to living my kind of life, and that I didn't have to die of hunger and sadness, all alone in my house, if I could just manage to show some nerve.

"I know it's hard for you to get up your courage," she said, fixing me with her eyes, as small and black as a pair of ripe olives. "You're a young lady, I can tell from your face."

"Natalia is a married woman," Beatrice interrupted. "But she lost her husband."

Dolores ignored her.

"What I mean is, you're a polite girl, probably one of them as never learned anything but praying and sewing. But you've got to face up to life with a bit of nerve or it'll swallow you whole. Come along and I'll introduce you to Doña Práxedes, and she's bound to hire you, with that virgin face of yours. You dance?"

Beatrice again answered for me, telling her about the tangos I had danced on my wedding day.

"There you go. Not like I'm telling you to go out and start walking the streets — wouldn't do that myself. She keeps a nice dance hall. The men that go there are clean, and they've got the wherewithal. They're honest men, too, working men, don't worry — not a thug or a spoiled brat among them. Doña Práxedes keeps guard like a German Shepherd, and Ignacio and Sebastián too, case anyone tries it on. You'll be with the rest of us girls, dolled up like a queen, nice dress, nice hair. When a man wants to dance with you, he'll give you a red token that he bought from Doña Práxedes. Stick the token in your bag and dance with the guy. One token, one dance. When the night's over, trade your tokens to the owner for the money you earned, and home you go."

I lowered my head, dying of shame to think that I'd reached the point where, instead of standing up and running away as any decent woman would have done, I was listening to what Dolores was saying. And it really didn't seem like such a bad idea.

"How long do you have to sew to pay for your coffee and roll?" she challenged me.

"All afternoon," I answered, barely moving my lips, not looking up.

"That's two tangos at the dance hall. Dance two songs with a man — maybe even a man you like — and you'll pay for your Sunday snack."

"Just dance?" asked Beatrice, also in a whisper.

"Just dance. If the guy wants anything else, and you want it too, talk it over with Doña Práxedes and she'll arrange it."

"What if you don't want to?"

"Just say the word, and so long! If he starts bugging you, Ignacio and Sebastián will come over and give him the chuck."

"They'll what?" asked Beatrice.

"Kick him out," I translated into Argentine for her.

Dolores licked the milk foam from her upper lip, stood up, smoothing her skirt over her hips, and looked me straight in the eye. "Come on, come with me. Let's go and see the dance hall. No obligation."

But I didn't go. Not that day, not the next day, not the day after.

Practically without my noticing, every time my gaze met Beatrice's while we sewed in my sitting room, I was thinking about the offer Dolores had made me. Just dance. Dance, which was what I loved most in the world, and earn enough to buy myself some meat now and then, probably even make myself a dress, if only so I could see myself in the mirror looking attractive.

A week went by, and when Beatrice was about to leave at supper time, I threw a glance her way so the other girls wouldn't see it. She understood, left with the others, gave them the excuse that she had forgotten her bag and came back to see what I wanted.

"Do you know how the girls dress when they go to Dolores' dance hall?" I asked, not daring to look straight at her.

"I went by there last Sunday," she said, and rapidly added, "Just for a minute, out of curiosity. They go nice. I mean, you can't see anything." She realized she was sticking her foot in it and tried to extricate herself. "Elegant. They wear satin or gauze dresses, short sleeves, skirts to the knee, a bit tight in an old-fashioned kind of way, you follow? Not like a really modern cut, low waist and off the shoulder."

"And their hair?"

"All sorts. Some of them are wearing it short now, cut *à la garçon*, like in the magazines, but most wear it long, in buns. And they wear a little bit of makeup — liner for their eyes, and red lipstick for cupid's-bow lips."

Almost a minute passed before either of us spoke. Then she asked me a question, and I instantly felt such warmth and such gratitude for her that I almost cried.

"What are you going to wear?" she asked, as if it were the most natural thing in the world, as if we had already discussed and decided everything. "If it has to be taken in or dyed or anything, you know you can count on me, as long as the others don't see us."

She hugged me and went home, where they were expecting her for supper. I went up to my bedroom, opened the wardrobe and, almost shocked at myself, took out my white satin wedding dress, the only nice dress I owned.

I'd been posing for five sessions already and he still hadn't let me see the painting. As soon as we finished a session, he'd throw a cloth over it, offer me a drink, and tell me that things were going well and I'd see it when it was finished.

I asked him several times whether he'd found the kind of doll he'd been looking for, and he finally told me, yeah, he'd found the perfect woman, the one who represented exactly what he was trying to get across, but it had cost him a ton of trouble to convince her, even though it was obvious she could use the cash. She was proud, he told me, and innocent, naïve, at the same time. Like an angel without wings who had to drag herself around on the ground like the rest of us. A flower in the mud, he called her, begging my pardon for being "a bit of a poet".

I felt all my muscles tense up. The only woman that description could fit was Natalia.

"Know what, *compadre?*" Nicanor said, wiping off his hands with a dirty rag that stank of paint thinner. "The two of you would make the perfect couple for a painting I've a mind to do. But she doesn't want to have anything to do with men. It cost me plenty to get her to come here, and she only does it when a girlfriend of hers comes along. Of course, we painters have a bad reputation, and half-witch painters like me, so much the worse."

"What do you mean, half-witch?" I asked.

"Just talk, as you might well imagine. My mother was a slave from Brazil, a mulatta, and she knew how to talk to the spirits. That's what she said, anyway. When I decided I wanted to be a painter — I was still just a kid — she made a spell for me, like the ones the *babalaos* or whatever do, so I could make the spirit of the people I paint enter the painting. I've never noticed anything. But people gossip, and lots of them are afraid to let me paint them, afraid I might steal their souls, I suppose." He laughed. A forced laugh, it seemed to me. "Lucky thing, rich people don't pay any attention to that rubbish, and thanks to my portraits of Buenos Aires high society I'm living a pretty good life. If I make it here, I'd like to move to Paris, or maybe New York."

"I used to want that, too," I said, quickly polishing off my drink.

"Not any more?"

"No."

"Dancing as well as you do, I think you'd have a good shot at it. A squeezebox player, friend of mine, is looking for a pair of dancers to go to Finland with him, to try their luck, because that's a country where people haven't grown tired of the tango, the way they have in France or Spain."

"Where's that?"

"It's in Europe, too, but all the way north. Nothing but ice and lakes and woods and so on. They say it's beautiful. Think about it, and if you like, I'll introduce you."

I stepped away from Nicanor and started pacing around the covered easel while he lit a cigarette. I didn't want my foolish hopes to be reborn: it had been hard enough for me to let go of my dreams, and I refused to believe in anything so absurd.

"My partner isn't up to it," I muttered, my back to him, looking at the unfinished portrait of a young lady from a nice home, dressed for a game of tennis. Nicanor's mother hadn't lied to him: he was capable of capturing someone's soul in a painting. That girl, silly as she was, looked about ready to come alive.

"Find yourself another one. Buenos Aires is full of women who are dying to dance."

I shook my head with a stubbornness that he couldn't have understood, that I couldn't even fully understand myself.

"If only you could see Natalia dance, you'd change your mind," the painter insisted.

"Natalia?" I wheeled to face him, and he must have noticed something in my eyes that left him confused for a few seconds. "You've seen Natalia dance? Where?"

He walked over to me, surprise still showing on his face, put his hand on my shoulder and led me to the back of his *atelier*, where another easel was covered with a cloth. He tore off the cloth with a flourish and turned the painting to face me.

"Are we talking about the same woman? Her?"

From the obscure depths of the canvas, Natalia's dark eyes stabbed at me like daggers.

"Where is she?"

He smiled a little condescendingly at me, as if he were disappointed that it had been so easy for him to convince me. He crushed the stub with his boot and took his time answering.

"If you let me paint the two of you together, I'll tell you."

"As you wish."

"You don't even have to pose. I have your features up here," he said, cupping his forehead. "All I want is your permission."

"For my part, you have it."

"She dances in El Divino, in La Boca."

"Doña Práxedes's nightclub?" My throat had gone dry and my voice sounded like a crow's.

"She's still a good girl."

"I know she is," I said. "Thanks, *compadre*."

That was the last time I ever saw Nicanor.

I spent my entire journey back to Buenos Aires doing sums, because I was stuck on the idea of figuring out exactly how long I had been gone and where it had happened to me, but the dates got all tangled up inside me and the only thing I knew for sure was that we had set sail from La Boca on the 29th of January, that autumn and winter were past, and that it must be spring now. Even though I'd first dropped anchor in Argentina years ago, it still seemed strange to me that October should be the start of good weather, that January should be summer, and May an autumn month.

Whenever I got tired of calculating dates and trying to remember the exact day we were shipwrecked, I would think about Natalia, and wonder whether Don Joaquín had died in the meantime and whether the company was paying her the salary that was hers by rights, even if it were only the puny widow's pension, because I was certain that after so much time they would have given us all up for dead.

I could have tried to send her word of my return through some other shipping company's offices after I finally reached Rio de Janeiro, but in some way that even I couldn't quite understand, I wanted to give her a surprise and at the same time get a chance to see her myself before she found out that I was still alive.

Sometimes I pictured myself arriving at the house on Necochea after dark: I'd be standing on the pavement across the street, away from the lamp, looking at the light in the bedroom, and maybe her shadow moving behind the blinds, too. Then I'd clack the knocker, and Natalia, upstairs, already in her nightdress and with her hair down, would put her hand to her chest, startled, and finally she'd come out on to the balcony to see who could be calling at that hour of the night. Then I'd take off my cap and stand under the street lamp, and she'd recognize me, shout with happiness, come running down the stairs, open the door to me, and we'd hug for the longest time. After that, I'd take her in my arms, and we'd go upstairs to the room, and while she was looking for something to give me to eat and drink, saying, "You're so skinny, Rojo, you'll have to put on some weight — how happy I am you're back!", I'd be looking around, overcome with joy to be in my house, in my bed, with my wife.

Other times, I'd find her in the morning, at the market, picking up her basket filled with freshly bought vegetables, wearing black for my sake, her face pale and haggard, her eyes lowered. Hearing my voice, she'd lift her eyes, startled, and slowly her gaze would fill with light, while her lips smiled. She'd drop the basket, and we'd hug right there, in front of everybody, who'd all suddenly start clapping and shouting, "It's Rojo! He's back! Nobody can beat Berstein!" Ever since I reached Argentina, nobody, not even I, had ever called me Bernstein. Too many letters, too hard to pronounce.

Some nights, when I wasn't able to sleep in whatever place I'd been given a job and a day's wages so I could keep on my journey, I would imagine returning to Necochea at night — I don't know why it was always at night that I was imagining this — and the house would be locked up and dark. I'd make the rounds of the cafés, the grocers, the shops, asking after her, but nobody knew anything, nobody remembered she was my wife. Finally somebody'd tell me her father had died and she'd gone away without leaving a forwarding address.

On nights like that, fear would make me break into a sweat, and I'd end up running wherever to swig a couple of drinks just so I could fall asleep, but lots of times the alcohol and the anguish of having lost her made me imagine worse things: that I'd return and find her with another man — a playboy who had money and a car, or a dagger-and-jaunty-hat *compadrito* like the guy at the wedding — or standing on a corner, street-walking, leaning against a doorjamb, with a cigarette in her hand and her eyes painted.

In Cádiz, our last port before putting in at Tenerife and heading back to America and sinking, I had met a drunken Bavarian soldier who had exactly that happen to him: returning from the war, the only survivor from his unit, he found his house empty. His wife had left for Munich. She was living with another man and expecting a baby.

"What did you do?" I asked him.

"What would you have done?"

"I don't know," I told him in all sincerity. "If your wife really thought she was a widow, well, it's better for a woman who's alone if she gets married, has a man to take care of her. But I'd have understood if you had killed them. Rage can blind a person."

He polished off his wine in one gulp, without replying, and laid his head down on his arm, on top of the bar.

"I'll never go back to Germany again," he spluttered.

"Come to Argentina. You can start over fresh there."

He fixed me with a blurry gaze, as if he barely registered who I was, what I was doing there, what I was talking about.

"I should have fallen at Verdun, like all the rest," he muttered to himself.

"Come with me," I said. "I'll walk you home. Think it over and tell me tomorrow what you've decided."

"Don't put yourself out, friend," he said with great difficulty, as if his own language were as hard for him to speak as a foreign tongue. "I'm already dead." He raised his head, looked at me with those sky-blue eyes, and smiled.

Ever since then I had carried that smile stuck inside me. Every time I thought about Natalia, all alone in La Boca for months and months, with no father, no family, no support from anyone, I imagined the worst. And I, who hadn't prayed in years, entered the first church I saw, knelt before the Virgin, and begged her to protect Natalia and to help me return to her and find her decent and good. Or at least to help me be strong enough not to kill her if she wasn't.

As I did every night, before the people started to arrive I looked down at my feet, because it always plucked up my courage to see them so pretty, so small, enclosed in the soft old dance shoes that had been worn down by so many hours of music. I had bought them the day after I made up my mind to come to the dance hall, in La Cañita, on Libertad between Sarmiento and Lavalle. When Dolores had seen me wearing my ankle boots, the only decent footwear I owned, she had laughed and led me there, even though it was Sunday, because La Cañita never closes. The poor people who no longer owned anything they could pawn, or who were sure they'd never have enough money to redeem their things, would all go to La Cañita to make a quick sale of anything they still owned. That's why things were so cheap there, if you could find something you needed.

My shoes had once belonged to someone named Grisela, a great tango dancer, according to the seller, who'd left Argentina to find success in Paris. He told me they'd bring me good luck as they had her, but the truth is, I bought them because the price was right. And they were the only ones my size.

I also bought some remnants of black gauze to make sleeves for the dress, and Beatrice helped me dye it and alter it, because the first day I went to the dance hall I wore my usual clothes — my black skirt and my good blouse, also black — and Doña Práxedes told me that, even if I was a widow, I didn't have to make such a show of it, for it would scare the men and ruin her business.

Dyeing my wedding dress was the worst thing I had ever done, even worse than what I did with Rojo, because, after all, what I did with Rojo was what a woman has to do with her husband. But lowering that lovely fabric into the pot of dye and watching what had been orange-blossom white grow greenish and filthy until turning finally black as coal, that was sorrow of a sort I could never explain. It was as if I myself were growing dirty, as if the little girl whose mother had rubbed brilliantine into her hair, the youngster whose grandfather had given her toys, the woman whose father had led her to the altar, were being dyed black along with the dress. For ever. Because once something turns black, it can never become white again.

When, alone at home, I looked into the mirror and saw myself in the fitted dress, with its gauze sleeves and high hem, black with a greenish sheen like a poor person's moiré, I felt a kind of dizziness. Because I saw a handsome woman. But it was no longer me.

And tonight, like every other night, I was looking at my shoes

« 143 »

and the silk shimmering on my legs and the reflection of my carmine lipstick like a red stain on the dull dance-hall mirror, and wondering who that stranger was, that woman who earned in an evening what I couldn't have made in a week before, and how she had got to that point, and especially, how she would keep going, because this couldn't last; in spite of the money I was making and the fact that most men came only to dance and I had never been put into a dangerous situation, this couldn't, shouldn't last.

I was thinking about what my grandfather or my father would say if they saw me like this, about the shame they would feel, as decent men, to see how low I had fallen, and I felt an urge to run away from that hall and go back to being what I had always been. But that would mean dying of hunger, burying my youth and my life within the walls of the house on Necochea, my only hope that one day, after I had been officially declared a widow, some honest man would show concern for me and want to lead me for a second time to the altar. And I didn't want that. Because that was even worse than what I was doing now, even if everybody else thought it more decent.

I was also recalling poor María Esther, the afternoons we used to spend at her house before we each got married, how she had asked me whether I didn't sometimes dream of dancing the tango in a theatre where men would watch me and bring me flowers. And bitter bile rose from the pit of my stomach when I looked around the dance hall and saw the dusty lampshade trim, the green velvet curtains blocking out the windows, the buffed marble café tables where men with tired eyes patiently awaited their turns, drinking cane liquor and rapping their tokens in time to the music. Then I lit a cigarette in memory of María Esther, wishing with all my heart that time could go in reverse, that we could be back in her house, smoking behind the curtains and imagining a future that was still ahead of us and that wasn't this.

Now my life was this dance hall and Urías' *atelier*, where I always went with Dolores. After he had persuaded me to let him paint me, he also proposed to make a double portrait, me and a partner, a portrait that would represent the tango, in which I would appear dancing with a friend of his. But I had said no, because I didn't want to embrace yet another stranger after the ones in the dance hall where I earned my living. If I had agreed to pose for him, it was because, deep down inside, I was still dreaming of the portrait that had never been — though my father wasn't around now to enjoy it, and I had no children to see it some day in a museum. And the painter was respectful and agreeable, though his skin was dark and mysterious things were said about him. But as soon as he finished the painting it would all be over, because I didn't want to insult the memory of Papá and because I didn't like to stand still there for hours while Urías stared fixedly at me, as if I were a jug or a fruit plate, as if he were extracting from me the last bit of life I had left, now that I was an orphan and a widow.

I was saving what I earned from those sessions in an old jam tin that I kept hidden in the courtyard, under the tree with yellow flowers. I didn't even know why, but it comforted me to know that I could do something with that money one day, whether or not I had any idea how to use it for the time being. If I ever truly tired of this life, I could sell the house on Necochea, take my savings and return to Spain, go to Vitoria or Valencia and perhaps open a haber-dasher's, or a flower shop. I had never made any plans for after the wedding, and now that all of a sudden and for the first time my life was in my own hands, I didn't know what to do with it.

I tried never to think of Rojo, of his white body at the bottom of the ocean, eaten by fish, of his empty eyes that had once been so blue and would now be nothing at all, of his big, strong hands that would now be two handfuls of dark seaweed.

But most of all, I tried not to think of Diego, of his voice, which I had scarcely ever heard, of his body, which was still scorched on to mine, of that burning gaze that had spoken so many things to me. I spent each night fearing that Yuyo might have told him where I was dancing and that he would come and see what I had turned into, and give me a red token and embrace me again. No, not like that. No. Anyone but him.

It took me months to make it back to Buenos Aires, but I did make it. And when, after all that suffering, I finally managed to reach Necochea one November night, a spring chill still in the air, I found the house closed up.

At first I felt nothing. One of my worst nightmares was coming true and I felt nothing. At most, an emptiness in my gut, a contraction in my right hand that made me seek relief in the hilt of my dagger, a throbbing in my temple.

I walked slowly towards the Gallego's shop, searching for an explanation of Natalia's absence. If Don Joaquín had died, maybe she had returned to Spain to ask for help from her family in Valencia. Or maybe she'd gone to spend the night at a girlfriend's house, if she was afraid of staying there alone. Or most likely she had gone out for a while with the Italian girls, to get some fresh air, and I would meet her on their stroll.

But it was already after ten. Even the shop was closed. La Boca was starting to fill with people coming to enjoy the night, tangos could be heard in every direction, women lurked in doorways and on street corners, men calmly strolled by jangling in their pockets the coins that they planned to spend. On Pedro de Mendoza the shops were still open and there was more of a family atmosphere, but I had a hunch I wasn't going to find Natalia there. And she couldn't be at church.

I decided to head up towards Progreso and Alegría. There were cafés around there where I might run into an acquaintance and ask about her, but I was ashamed to be seen so desperate, so lost — a poor man returning from a shipwreck, having to make the rounds of the cafés to ask after his wife in the middle of the night.

On the way, in amongst the other men who were on the hunt, I drank a glass or two of cane liquor to screw up my courage, and I slowly started to notice that people were keeping their distance from me, so the beast must have been baring its fangs and showing its face through mine, heating my heart along the way.

Three days went by before I made up my mind to go and look for her. When a doll like Natalia starts dancing in Doña Práxedes's dance hall, it means she's desperate, and nobody wants to be seen like that. But I had to go and see her. Had to go and take her away from all that, no matter how. Had to tell her I loved her, tell her I'd spent nearly a year waiting for the right moment to let her know, to tell her she could trust me.

The dance hall was on Alegría, and from what I'd been told it was in even worse shape than it had been years before. I had always known it crowded with single men who never allowed the girls a minute's rest, snatching them from one another without even giving them time to wipe the sweat that drenched their clothes. It frightened me to imagine Natalia there, innocent as she was, all alone, no-one to help her but Doña Práxedes' pair of bruisers, those two old broad-assed Gallegos who couldn't stand up to anyone remotely experienced at handling a dagger.

The streets were packed, as always on a Saturday night, more so tonight, what with the All Saints' Day just over and people wanting to have a spree.

I was getting closer and closer to Alegría, feeling my feet grow heavier with every step, trying to grit my teeth so nobody'd notice what I had going on inside, coming apart at the seams with desire for her and at the same time with sorrow and shame that it had to be in that place, in this way.

In spite of what I thought I felt when we embraced at the wedding, I knew she didn't love me. She had never asked Yuyo about me, it hadn't occurred to her to seek me out when she was left alone, and she had found the dance hall a better solution than turning to me, though I would have given my life for her gladly if she'd asked me.

What would I do now if I entered El Divino and she snubbed me?

But there I was. I smoothed my jacket, set my fedora on the sill for a minute while I brushed my hair back with both hands, straightened my kerchief, and entered the hall.

Nearing Progreso, minutes before midnight, I saw two men leave a building and start walking slowly past me. I recognized one of them. A fellow named Quinquela, a painter, one of the regulars who met at the Bar Unión. I remembered his name because my father-in-law told me once, a long time ago, that he wanted to commission a portrait of Natalia if his carpenter's shop did well, so our children could see what their mother looked like when she was twenty. Quinquela knew her through Don Joaquín, but I wasn't sure if it was a good idea for me to ask him, because most likely he didn't know anything, and he'd find out that I was out looking for her and that my wife had got away from me, taking advantage of me being off at sea.

They stopped under a street lamp to roll a cigarette. I waited, too, trying to hear what they were saying.

"Urías is amazing," said the other guy, a stranger to me. "I think what he's doing is a little outdated now, but you almost expect his figures to start breathing. That girl is a real beauty."

"Indeed. Natalia is the best of La Boca. Her father wanted to commission her portrait, but he didn't have the cash. Now it's done. It's the tango in the form of a woman."

"And a man, Quinquela. That couple would be the rage of Europe. And the painting is . . . tragic, don't you think? Gives you the shivers."

Quinquela patted the other fellow, who had just lit his cigarette, on the shoulder.

"Don't go philosophical on me, Montero. It's a good painting, a very good one, to be sure, but it's just a piece of canvas, like our own."

Hearing them mention Natalia, I made up my mind. It had to be my Natalia: few women in the district shared that name.

"Excuse me," I said, approaching them, cap in hand. "I happened to overhear you, and, since I've been away at sea for months and just got back . . ."

Both turned to look at me, curious.

"My name is Berstein. Natalia is my wife."

We shook hands, and I saw them exchange a glance I didn't like.

"I'd like to take a peek at that portrait," I said, trying to keep them from noticing the rage that was welling up in me. They had said something about a man being with Natalia.

"It is not a typical portrait. It's a painting in which Nicanor Urías depicted a couple dancing the tango. He has it in his *atelier*, right here, number 13. If you knock now, you might still find him."

Quinquela was looking me over thoroughly, as if to examine me. "You're a sailor, aren't you?"

"Boatswain on a freighter."

"Come see me some day. I'd like to paint your portrait."

I quickly took my leave and looked for the number he had mentioned. I clacked the knocker and, to my surprise, the door opened immediately. A small man with a smile on his face, perhaps mulatto, was handing me a blue scarf.

"Excuse me," he said when he saw me, changing his expression. "Some friends just left and I thought they were coming back for something they forgot."

"I want to see the painting," I said, not greeting him.

"The painting?"

"That tango painting, the one your friends are talking about."

His expression hardened and he tried to close the door on me.

"It's after hours, and the painting's not for sale."

I shoved the door open with my shoulder, took out my dagger and pushed the painter inside.

"I said I want to see it. Now."

His dark face lost its colour. Never taking his eyes off me, he backed down the hall to a large, well-lit room that held only one painting, in the middle of the room, on an easel.

I didn't have to ask him if that was the one.

On the cloth, Natalia, eyes half closed with pleasure, a smile on her lips that I'd never seen her wear, was embracing that *compadrito* from the wedding, who, with his eyes also half closed, was resting his hand on her waist in a possessive gesture.

It was true. I almost expected them to breathe.

There, before my very eyes, that man was embracing my wife, and she gave herself over to him as she never had to me. Just the two of them, and the damn tango, ignoring the whole world around them.

I sprang at the canvas, dagger in hand, but the painter stepped in and, hardly realizing what I was doing, I plunged the blade into his chest.

"No!" he cried. "No!"

I don't know if he meant I shouldn't destroy his painting or if he was talking about himself.

"Natalia is mine!" I shouted, so he'd understand. "She's my wife!"

The room was spinning around me, blood was pounding in my ears. I felt it throb through me, like the machine room of the *Star*, and gush to my right hand, which had just pulled the dagger from the painter's chest. The painting lay on the floor. Urías had fallen on top of it, and now he was trying to roll aside so that the blood oozing out of him wouldn't stain his work.

"It's the best I've ever done," he groaned. "Don't hurt it. Natalia hasn't done anything wrong. She didn't even pose with Diego for the painting. I painted them from memory, I swear." His voice was losing strength and he had started to sob.

"Where is she?"

"Help me. Find a doctor. I won't turn you in, you have my word."

"Where is she?"

Seeing that he didn't want to answer me, I grabbed the painting.

"No!" he cried again.

With the dagger I ripped the canvas in half, cutting Natalia away from the embrace that was burning me up inside.

The painter was moaning like a little girl and trying to close his wound with his open hands.

"Where is she?" I asked again, holding the blade to his throat.

He opened his eyes wide and suddenly gave in.

"At El Divino, on Alegría, like every night."

I grabbed the two halves of the canvas, folded them up and stuck them in the waistband of my trousers.

"Don't hurt Natalia," I heard when I was nearly at the door.

I don't know why, but that made me laugh, and when I reached the door of the dance hall I was still cackling with laughter.

Doña Práxedes was complaining that it was a slow night. I heard her mention it to the other girls when I let go of my partner for a moment to drink a glass of water; I even heard her send Ignacio and Sebastián outside to talk up the dance hall to the men who were standing undecided around the door or strolling from café to café trying to choose between them.

I hadn't stopped dancing all night long. I couldn't even remember how many tangos I'd danced already, constantly changing partners, because if there was anything Doña Práxedes wouldn't stand for, it was a guy who "manopolized" a girl, as she put it. My feet had started to hurt and a sweet pain was also spreading from my legs up to my waist. I would have loved to sit down for a bit and drink something cool, but as soon as one song ended, even before my partner let go of me, another man would be standing there, token in hand, eager to embrace me and give himself over to the tango.

Sometimes I felt sorry for them, so lonely, squeezing a few minutes of happiness from their hard and hopeless lives, or a few minutes of oblivion, which was what almost all of them sought.

When I first started working in the dance hall, I had feared that they just wanted to touch a woman's body, that they'd try stepping over the line until Ignacio and Sebastián would have to rudely toss them out, leaving me feeling dirty and guilty; but later on, night by night, I came to realize that the only thing most of them wanted to do was dance: to feel protected, sheltered, to have someone to embrace them while they thought about their distant girlfriends or mothers or nothing at all, simply letting themselves go, feeling the music, the warmth, the companionship, before they had to go home to their poor solitary rooms and wretched jobs in one of the richest countries in the world, to which they, like my father, had immigrated in the hope that luck would smile on them.

This night, despite being hot and exhausted, I felt good. Ridiculously, I felt a bit like a sister of mercy, an angel descended to earth to comfort them; a wingless black angel who could still offer them a hint of paradise.

Then I saw him, and everything stood still, even though I kept dancing.

My heart sank when I saw Diego talking to Doña Práxedes, lavishing on her one of his nice-boy smiles that lit up the whole dance hall, as if they had turned up all the lamps.

Dazzled, she smiled too, showing her gold tooth and nervously patting the curls of her dyed hair. The girls who were sitting around the bar without partners also started straightening their dresses, lighting cigarettes, and fluttering their eyelashes at him, hoping to be picked.

I wanted to die, and when he finally parted from Doña Práxedes and walked towards us, I had to hold tight to my partner to keep from falling down. At that very moment, with a final flourish, the squeezebox stopped and the song was over. My partner stuck his hand in his waistcoat pocket to offer me another token, but Diego interrupted.

"It's my turn, friend," he said without taking his eyes off me. The man walked away and I was left there, face to face with Diego, trembling.

"May I have this dance?" In his outstretched hand lay a fistful of red tokens; on his lips, a tense smile.

I glanced at Doña Práxedes, who assented with a nod, and the tokens disappeared into my bag.

A moment later, as soon as the violin struck a chord and the bandoneón began to wail, everything else disappeared. We were dancing. Dancing in a fog. I felt his body so close to mine, his warmth, his manly scent like a sudden fragrance of red geraniums after it rains. We were one, and nothing else mattered. We were the tango, Diego and I. And then I thanked God for having brought us to this land, and I felt everything had been worth it — the deaths of María Esther, my father and Rojo; the poverty, the shame, the sorrow — for it had all led me to this moment, and life could never bring me anything better than this.

When I felt Natalia in my arms, after all those months of loneliness and anger, everything immediately vanished. I made my peace with the world the moment the tango started up, and I, who had been coming to terms for so long with the fact that my dreams would never come true, suddenly began making plans for the future.

While we danced, I, clinging to an angel who elevated me above the misery of this life, was dreaming of Europe. We'd go to Finland, that beautiful, faraway country of blue lakes and ice flowers, and dance there for ever, spreading the tango like an incurable disease throughout the dancers of the land. As soon as I felt sure my voice wouldn't tremble, I would tell Natalia about it, whispering into her ear, like a good-luck spell. Now that we were together, nothing could separate us.

With my eyes closed, feeling her trembling body against mine, everything seemed possible, and I let myself be carried away by the magic of the tango, forgetting the poverty of the dance hall, the immigrant district that surrounded us, the dashed hopes of all those who looked on us with envy. We'd earned the right to be happy, after all we'd been through.

No-one interrupted us when the song ended. We waited, in our embrace, looking at one another eye to eye, for the music to start up again, then went on dancing, until at last, stopping by a column, she suddenly raised her face, and I kissed her.

We kissed each other.

My entire life's purpose had been to get me to this moment. My entire life would end there, at her lips, at her scent, at this woman who was now part of me, who was me, but purified, elevated, perfect, the person I never knew I could aspire to be.

We kissed for so long that I finally noticed the silence that had fallen on the dance hall and lifted my gaze.

At the door, with his hand in his waistcoat pocket and something tucked into his trousers, the red-haired German was looking at us, wild-eyed.

Natalia had her back turned to the entrance and couldn't see him, but she noticed how I stiffened, and she looked into my eyes in fear.

I kissed her again, in desperation, almost in fury.

Then she cried out, her eyes opened wide in surprise, and her body went limp in my arms.

I saw them as soon as I entered the dance hall. I hardly had time to notice the filth all over the place, the whores leaning their elbows on the bar, the crowd of sailors, washed and combed, still stinking of ship fuel and man-sweat, the old madam with the red hair who hunkered behind the till, looking around for the thugs who could toss me out of there, not knowing that even God Himself on high, with all his angels and devils, couldn't have done anything to stop me now.

Because they were kissing each other. Right there in front of everyone.

The painter had been lying when he told me they hadn't posed together. The whole district must have known by now that Natalia was a whore, that this guy fondling her here in public was her pimp, that there was nothing else I could do but kill the two of them, or else I'd never be able to let anyone look me in the face again.

But I thought all that later. At that moment, I believe I didn't think anything. The slick-haired *compadrito* looked up and went pale. Natalia never saw me. I saw them kissing, crossed the dance floor in two bounds, like an eagle swooping down to rend its prey, and buried the dagger in her back.

I didn't want to see her eyes. I didn't want to see the shining black eyes, so sweet, that had been my perdition. I didn't want to hear her plead for mercy for herself or for him either. I didn't want to be weak and forgive her. All I wanted was to rid myself of the grief that was growing and growing inside me, leaving me deaf and blind, rending me like the claws of a wild beast.

He took her in his arms, leaned against the column, and slowly slid down to the floor, never glancing my way, looking only at her, caressing her hair, whispering into her ear.

I started stomping and kicking him while sobs and wails rose around me. I knew my time was up, that the house thugs would be back any second, that they'd call the police, that the whores would fall on me and try to scratch out my eyes with their nails. But I was hoping that this guy would be man enough to stand up and draw his dagger, fight for his life, maybe even kill me.

But he wasn't.

I had to stab him lots of times. Even so, he never let go of Natalia.

I threw the two pieces of painting on top of them, then turned around, expecting to see the sheen of a blade. But everybody was just staring at me, frightened, shrinking into the nooks and crannies of the hall.

"Cowards! Fairies!" I think I shouted.

Nobody made a move to stop me. I looked at the two of them one last time, lying at my feet, in a puddle of dark blood that was spreading across the worn, scratched parquet floor. I knelt down by Natalia and took her wedding ring. There was nothing left to do there. Whatever might happen afterwards had nothing to do with me.

I wiped the dagger clean on the green velvet curtain, taking my time, under the gaze of a hundred pairs of eyes, and walked out into a cool spring morning that smelled of the sea. I was finished, but I was clean. I smiled.

FIVE

I am pretty sure, Rodrigo, that you were trembling that night, that something stronger than your will had brought you there, to a place where you had been before but where you hadn't yet found what you were seeking. Habit had dragged you back to the little house on Necochea, which once, in a different century, had been painted blue, though it was now no more than an empty shell of what once might have been the start of a new life.

As you recalled, weeds were growing on the front steps, the windows were coated with dust and boarded up, and there was nothing there to confirm the existence of the mysterious woman you had met in Central Europe months earlier. But it was November now, spring was in the damp port air, in the fog that shrouded everything, and the district was bathed in nostalgia, in the blurry memories of nights on the town, music and drink, even though there was nothing now but solitude and sadness.

You vaguely thought you'd like to have seen that street in earlier days, and you stood there staring in fascination at the rosy, intermittent light of the street lamp, trying to look through it to imagine the gas lamp that once lit the corner of Olavarría street. Curiously, you felt on that night that you could see the past, as if the reality around you were some tenuous gauze veil, barely covering some other, truer, more intense reality; as if that bygone time still existed there, pooling in the dark doorways, hiding from everyday passers-by, only to reveal itself in all its splendour to those who were worthy.

You heard her steps before you saw her silhouette, diffused by the fog that rose from the river. A few slow footsteps, women's shoes, high heels rapping on the damp asphalt to a beat that matched the rhythm of your blood.

For some seconds all there was were those slow, almost fearful footsteps drawing closer to the place, to the sealed door where you were still waiting, what for you didn't really know. Then a sudden desire to flee, to find a well-lit café where the tango would be playing and women would be sitting at their tables, waiting for a good dancer. You were afraid to stay there in the fog, listening to footsteps that seemed to be drawing nearer and nearer, or perhaps deeper and deeper within you. Your right hand slid to your side, tried to close around the hilt of a dagger you had never owned, then moved away again, leaving you bewildered and frightened at yourself, while inside you a stranger's voice was shouting how dangerous it might be to stay there unarmed. But the idea of leaving scared you more, knowing that you might be about to find what you had so long sought.

Then you saw her: a graceful woman, blond, nearly platinum blond, walking slowly down to the piers. A cigarette's glow lit her mouth. Your fear vanished without a trace, but your gaze was trapped by the figure approaching you on the empty street.

You felt a twinge of disappointment, because she wasn't the woman you had been waiting for, yet something in the way she moved, something in the way she spontaneously held her cigarette by the tips of her fingers, close to her thigh, something in the swish of her footsteps made you suddenly stand up straight and accept her presence in that place, as if she were also a mirage from the past, a shred rent from the fog of time.

I know, Milena, that you expected to find nothing there; as a sensitive yet sensible woman, accustomed to seeing the world and to fixing all sorts of situations, always on your own, you never expected that time could be smashed to shards this way, like a mirror. Yet an uncontrollable impulse beyond your will had brought you to Necochea on a damp November night, ready to suffer one more defeat, ready to admit to yourself, hours later in your hotel room, that the ghost that had kept you from sleeping was merely an absurd obsession born of exhaustion and solitude.

The taxi had left you further up the street, on the corner of Pinzón, because you wanted to walk a while through the nearly transparent fog that was rising from the port as in an old movie, though boats no longer blew their horns in the harbour and silence now spread everywhere. A few paces later, already regretting your desire, you decided to light a smoke, walk to the house on Necochea that you knew so well, and continue to Caminito, where you might find a squeezebox player and a good tanguero, the two things that linked those two worlds, those two times, in the vague, ridiculous hope that he might be there with his shockingly black hair and his green eyes, as he had been there in the distant snow-covered city where you had lost him.

You could make out his silhouette from far away, haloed by the dim light of the street lamp that blinked on and off as if in its death throes, standing in for the gas lamp that had witnessed a night-time serenade in an era that wasn't yours: the silhouette of a man, in coat and hat, black against the light, blurred by the fog that encircled his feet in a diaphanous mist.

Your steps slowed down. The cigarette stub trembled in your hand. It wasn't him — and yet. There was something in the tension of his body, in the angle of his fedora, in his just being there, standing by the door of the little blue house, looking at you.

The blond woman approached you with uncertain steps, as if trying to recognize you through the shadows, and you made a tentative motion in her direction, careful not to startle her. Her cigarette flew aside, peppering the street with golden sparks, and then there was a pause, a long silence, a deep gaze through which each of you sought confirmation.

It was as if you had met each other in your dreams, in an urban landscape but a false one, halfway between two existences, between two planes of reality.

That is why it didn't seem strange to you, Milena, to extend your hand to the stranger, who shook it firmly, perhaps to make sure of your existence.

"This isn't the first time you have come here, either," said the man, and it was not a question.

The statement didn't surprise you, because by then, without even realizing it, you had already crossed over into a borderland where anything could happen.

"Hope springs eternal, you know," you replied, knowing that he would understand. "I suppose I'll never meet him, but I look for him here because there's nowhere else to look. And you?"

"Same with me. I've seen her portrait in the museum and I know it's impossible. Her name was Natalia. They painted her back around 1920."

"Mine was Diego. The same date is on his portrait." You lit another smoke and stared at the boarded-up windows. "I don't sleep well, you know? Something makes me keep coming back here. For nothing."

"Yes. Me too."

"Shall we enter?"

Your question made the man turn to look at you, amazed and disquieted.

"How? Do you have the key?"

Ignoring his question, your fingers felt under a loose tile on the bottom step and found a rusted iron key. You had stood many times in front of this house, on every trip you took to Buenos Aires, but you had never felt such certainty, it had never even occurred to you that you could try to open the door with the key that, you now knew, had always been hiding under the step.

Without a word you fitted key to lock, and after a struggle the door gave way, opening on to the dark interior of the house.

A smell of dust and old house assailed you both, like an almost tangible presence that must have been waiting years for the chance to escape its prison.

"There can't be anybody in here." Your soprano voice sounded muffled, as if you had suddenly lost the determination that had led you to open the door.

"No. I suppose not. But perhaps it will help us to sleep better. To understand. Don't you think?"

The man lit a match and preceded you into a long hallway that smelled like a musty crypt. To your right, a staircase rose into the darkness of the upper floor. To your left, the kitchen was barely discernible beneath the ancient grime and the pots and pans abandoned to their fate. The two of you saw an old-fashioned sitting room with a gutted divan, a cobweb-laced dining room with an almost fossilized layer of dust over every surface, a sideboard mirror smashed to scintillating bits that reflected the match's wavering light, empty bottles.

You walked out into the overgrown courtyard. In contrast to the darkness and the foetid smell of the interior, this seemed like paradise. You both breathed deep, looking around at the tall weeds that had begun to bud. A tall tree, studded with yellow flowers, covered half the sky. From one of its branches dangled a stiff, thick rope with a hangman's noose.

You were hardly surprised, though shivers went up your spines.

"What was that, shining for a second on the ground?" Your white hand, lined with bluish veins, rested on the sleeve of his black coat.

Another match. Picking your way with difficulty through the bushes that caught on his trouser legs, on your fine stockings.

"Careful. The plants are very dry."

At the end of the rope, on the ground: a rusted tin that had once contained quince jam, surrounded by the scattered bones of a human skeleton. You opened the tin with trembling hands by the light of a mobile phone. Inside, a few Argentinian bills, brittle with age, two stained black-and-white postcards, and a gold wedding ring.

The postcards showed views of the Golden Roof of Innsbruck

and the Old Town Hall of Landsberg on market day. Among the people in the image, to the left, enclosed in a circle drawn in ink, were a diminutive man pushing a tinsmith's or knife-grinder's cart and a little boy with long, fair hair who stared unblinking into the camera.

By the ghostly light of the mobile phone you looked one another in the face, slowly understanding in the other's eyes the story behind this house, and at the same time your own stories from the moment when, far from here, you had each discovered the passion of the tango in a being who couldn't be. But that was not enough. You both knew that a piece was missing, the essential piece for bringing to a close a story that had been cut short eighty years before.

Slowly, without making up your minds to do it, you drew closer to one another. A pale hand caressed an unshaven cheek; lips lightly brushed blond, nearly platinum locks.

You looked at each other for a long time, in the thickening fog, by the tree with yellow flowers,

. . . in Natalia's house, which I never got to enter, except on the night of the serenade . . .

. . . in my house, in the very courtyard where I bathed on the morning of my wedding day . . .

. . . in the house on Necochea, where so often, on so many trips, you had each waited for the miracle to occur.

Leaving behind the bones and the tin and the courtyard and the weeds, you left the house, at a leisurely pace, hand in hand, looking at one another from the corner of your eyes from time to time as if to find in the other a presence that you were beginning to guess was there.

You wandered through the dark and empty fog-lined streets, letting yourselves be led by vague memories that were not yet your own, while time folded around you, gas lamps appeared and disappeared with every step, and somewhere a distant squeezebox played a melody that you both sensed could not really be.

You paused when you got to the street named W. Villafañe, formerly known as Alegría, in front of a modern shipping company that, at that late hour, was closed and had the lights off. Nevertheless the music rose in all its power from behind the doors, and you both knew that, at this instant, anything was possible and that the front door would swing open if you touched it, showing you a world that you could scarcely imagine. Perhaps Diego and Natalia would be waiting for you right there, in the ineluctable spot to which you had been called by so many dreams in so many hotels.

After looking at each other for a few seconds, you pushed the door and it swung in.

For a moment you believed you saw the crystal chandeliers, the dusty lampshade trim, the long green velvet curtains, the marble café tables, the musicians in black suits and bow ties — and you even felt the rush of hot air and the smell of drink and sweat-drenched couples dancing the tango in the middle of the hall.

A second later you were in a dusty warehouse, surrounded by the debris of days gone by, in the company of ghosts.

And something inside each of you let out a scream as it was ripped from your body, while your hands and lips recognized other hands and other lips, the ones they had lost in that very place, while the tango played.

We felt so sorry for you, Rodrigo, Milena, so very sorry. You couldn't have known we had been waiting nearly a century for this reunion, that we had been floating, alone and lost, in the shadows while the world changed, trusting that some day, some night, some milonga, the sound of the tango would come back and allow us to return to the place where it had all begun. And now we were back, though nothing was the same, in other bodies, with other names, but we had done it thanks to you two, who were now but a cry lost in the limbo that we had already started to forget.

"Diego?" I whispered, in a voice that wasn't mine.

"Natalia?" he said, looking at me as if for the first time, with his fiery eyes, no longer green.

We kissed for a long, long time, while the fog outside grew thicker in the dance hall of red tokens, in the streets that once were ours, that bore witness to our beginning and our end.

"What shall we do now?" Natalia whispered in my ear, not stirring from my embrace, still trembling.

"Dance, my darling," I told her. "Dance the tango."

ACKNOWLEDGEMENTS

I want to thank all the friends and colleagues who, in one way or another, have helped me in the writing and rewriting of these pages.

To Gustavo and Luciana, who allowed us to stay in their apartment in Buenos Aires for several unforgettable days; to Petra Möderle, who, despite the excess luggage, generously brought me books, maps and photocopies from her stay in Argentina; to Mario and Ruth of Libertango Innsbruck, who encouraged us to enrol in tango classes, even though we unfortunately did not keep it up and I now only dance with words; to Biggi Steurer of the Textmusik in der Romania Archive of Innsbruck University, who waited more than a year for me to return the books and discs he had lent me; to all the specialists on the tango and the social life of Buenos Aires whose texts (printed and online) I have read with such pleasure: if, despite their erudition, there are errors in the novel, the fault is all mine; to Homero Manzi for the tango lyrics that open this novel, which I discovered after I had begun writing it; to Sabine März-

Lerch and my Landsberg friends, for their enthusiasm and their city; to Chavi Azpeitia, who extricated me from the labyrinth of narrators in which I had lost myself; once again to Ruth and Mario, to Gertrut, Wolfram and Michael, the best readers one could hope for, for their friendship and valuable suggestions.

To Klaus, my husband, for his enthusiasm, his strength, and his unconditional support.

And, of course, to the maestro Julio Cortázar, always.